GARRET'S GAMBIT

Bullard's Battle
Book #4

Dale Mayer

GARRET'S GAMBIT (BULLARD'S BATTLE, BOOK 4)
Dale Mayer
Valley Publishing

Copyright © 2021

This is a work of fiction. Names, characters, places, brands, media, and incidents either are the product of the author's imagination or are used fictitiously. Any resemblance to actual events, locales, or persons, living or dead, is entirely coincidental.

ISBN-13: 978-1-773363-28-8
Print Edition

Books in This Series:

About This Book

Welcome to a new stand-alone but interconnected series from Dale Mayer. This is Bullard's story—and that of his team's. All raw, rough, incredibly capable men who have one goal: to find out who was behind the attack on their leader, before the attacker, or attackers, return to finish the job.

Stay tuned for more nonstop action as the men narrow down their suspects … and find a way to let love back into their own empty lives.

Stronger than he had any right to be after the plane explosion and still angry about it all, Garret's seriously unimpressed to fly to London to speak with an ex-fiancée who'd screwed him over with his own brother. But she had information on his missing brother, who was a link to the plane crash that sent Garret into the ocean.

Yet Astra, not Amy, waits in London for Garret, to explain the little she knows, hoping he'll let go of some of his resentment and help her look for her sister, Amy—who disappears just before Garret's arrival. Some coincidence there. Then her sister hasn't faced the music for any of her actions in a long time. Today is no different. Too bad Amy and Garret hadn't broken up much earlier. It might have given Astra a chance with the man she has loved since forever.

Still, if finding Astra's sister leads Garret to finding his brother, who might be able to give them answers regarding the sabotaged plane, then Astra's happy to play the game. However, it's not that easy, as the men who failed to kill the two team members are still looking for their chance to finish the job. And to take out anyone who is close by ...

Sign up to be notified of all Dale's releases here!

https://smarturl.it/DaleNews

CHAPTER 1

G ARRET BALDERSON AND Kano walked toward the front doors of the airport. They carried only duffel bags with them, and Garret hadn't even had a chance to regroup from his last trip, still dealing with the aftermath of his coma, yet powering through that too. But he was here now, walking into the same airport that he'd only left a few minutes before. He never made it out of the parking lot before being informed of his newest destination. Once on the plane and in the air, he finally started to relax. Without realizing, he slipped into a deep restorative sleep.

Kano shook Garret gently, as the plane began to descend. "Okay, time to get busy. So, how bad is your relationship with Amy?"

"It sucks," he said grimly.

"Wonderful," he said. "She didn't ask for you specifically. Is that important?"

"No, she wouldn't," he said. "Not unless it was a dire emergency."

"Well, with your brother missing, it potentially is."

Granted, they worked on different teams for Bullard but, with compartmentalized ops, there wasn't any crossover, unless one team had to bail out another. Garret didn't respond because he, Amy, and his brother, Gregg, had all been caught up in a nasty triangle that ended with Garret

1

being the odd man out, once he discovered his fiancée was having an affair with his brother.

As far as he knew, his relationship with Gregg was still strong but maybe not. Maybe Garret just used that as a way to keep his mind clear and to help his heart disengage.

As they walked out into the hazy, rainy day, Garret stopped and sighed. "I wonder if London has ever once looked sunny with clear skies?"

"Not any time that I've landed here," Kano replied. "Come on. Let's grab a rental."

"Isn't it already arranged?"

"Supposedly but waiting on confirmation, as my messages download. We seem to be having some network trouble since we landed." Just then both of their phones went off, showing the updates that had come in. Kano looked at his phone and said, "Oh, we have a ride here waiting for us."

"As long as it's not Amy," Garret said, with feeling. "I'm not quite ready for that."

"Maybe not," he said. "Charles sent a car."

Garret stopped, looked at him, and said, "Charles? How did that work out? Are we staying with him?"

Kano shrugged. "Potentially. Have no idea as yet."

"That means MI6 is already aware that we're here," Garret said.

"No surprise there," Kano said. "I'm sure they flagged us as soon as we came through security."

"And yet no need for them to know," he said.

"Doesn't matter that there is or isn't. We're on their home turf, and we sometimes do property damage while we're here," Kano said, with half a smile.

"I don't really think that's a fair assessment," Garret said, with a chuckle of his own.

"No, you're right," he said. "We *always* do property damage when we're here."

"Not intentionally though," Garret clarified. "It's not like we intend to leave a path of destruction in our wake."

"No, but, whenever we're here, we're after bad guys, and they are the ones causing damage."

"A much better way of looking at it," he said, with a smirk. When they made their way outside, they saw a black luxury car waiting, its driver leaning against the door, his arms crossed.

They stopped, looked at him, and Kano said, "Ah, it's Jonas."

"Wow," Jonas said, walking toward them. "Did you think it would be anybody else?"

"Don't you have somebody else better to babysit?" Garret said, complaining.

"You land in my country, then you land on my turf," he replied in a reasonable voice. But his jaw muscle twitched.

"We thought somebody else was coming to get us."

"Maybe, but you're not going anywhere before you talk to me," Jonas said, and his tone brooked no argument.

So they stood at the side of the vehicle. "Here and now?" Garret asked.

"Sure, and then I can drop you off wherever you want to go."

"Of course you can," Garret said, with a sigh. The three men got inside, Jonas driving, with Garret and Kano taking the back seat, but the car was not moving.

"What are you here for?" Jonas asked.

"To talk to my ex-fiancée," Garret said in a hard voice. "You got a problem with that?"

3

Jonas twisted around in the front seat to look back at him. "Why the hell would you want to do that?"

"Apparently she has some information for me," he said. "I don't know if I believe her or not because I don't trust her."

"Nice relationship," he said.

"Yeah, maybe."

"That's Amy, huh?"

Frowning, Garret looked at him and asked, "How do you know that?"

"Hey, we've got sources too," Jonas replied.

"Sure, you do," Garret said, rolling his eyes. "The bottom line is, I'm not exactly sure what it is she wants to tell us or even if it's coming from her or someone else. But, either way, what difference does it make to you?"

"Well, for one thing, she's gone missing," he said, "and her sister's here, raising hell."

"What do you mean, *Amy's gone missing?*"

Again came that look from the front seat. "Just what I said. She's gone missing."

"Who reported her missing?"

"Again, just what I said. Her sister," Jonas replied. "Do you know her?"

"Astra, yes," Garret said. "I do."

"Good, because we need to talk to her, and she's not being very cooperative."

"Huh, it's almost like she knows you," Garret said.

"Funny. We need to find out if she knows anything about her sister's disappearance."

"If she's the one who called it in, then she's probably already told you everything she knows," he said.

Kano looked at Garret. "Who is this Astra?"

GARRET'S GAMBIT

"Amy's kid sister," he said.

"How much of a kid sister?"

"Four years maybe," he said. "I don't remember exactly. She was there when it all blew up. I told her that I was walking, and she just shrugged and said that she would too."

"Interesting take on it."

"Yeah, Amy and Astra don't get along very well," he said. "So it's interesting that she's the one who called it in."

"Maybe," Kano said.

"Let's go have a little talk with her, shall we?" Jonas said.

"What are we, inseparable now? But, if I don't have a choice, then I don't have a choice," Garret said. "Let's get on with it. But, Jonas, it would have been nice if I'd had a choice."

"Dream on," he said. "You know how we feel about giving you too much of a choice."

"You didn't have to meet us here."

"Not to worry," he said. "We'll drop you off at Charles's later."

Garret settled in his seat and said, "So you'll put Charles in the spotlight over this too?"

"Of course not," he said. "The way we get along with Charles is that he keeps us in the loop."

"And did he tell you that we were coming?"

"Doesn't matter if he did or didn't," Jonas said cheerfully, as they pulled up in front of a hotel. "We would have heard from other channels."

Garret looked at the hotel and asked, "Astra's here?"

"Yes."

"And you expect our presence to loosen her tongue?"

"It's worth a try," Jonas said.

"You're not treating her like the family of a missing person, which I find interesting. You treat all your crime victims this way?"

"Why would she be a victim?"

"Well, her sister's missing. Yet you think she has intel that she's not giving up? Isn't that counterproductive? The sister would want you to find Amy. So what gives, Jonas?"

"Yeah, I don't understand that either," Kano said. "Something else is behind this."

"There is," Garret said, "no doubt. But Jonas here, he likes to play things close to the vest."

"It's the only way to operate," Jonas said.

"Not true," Garret said.

"With you guys, it is," Jonas said. "You are nothing but consistent—consistently right in our way."

"I wouldn't worry about it," Garret said. "It's not likely to stay that way."

"Says you, but we need something to break here."

"Twenty-four hours already gone by?"

"Almost," Jonas admitted.

"Well, I'm glad that she's deserving of at least that much attention," he said. "Anybody mention my brother?"

At that, Jonas got out of the vehicle and leaned down, looking at him with a frown. "What about your brother?"

"Well, apparently he's missing," Garret said. "That's why I'm here to talk to Amy. She supposedly had information on his disappearance."

At that, Jonas started to swear.

"What's the matter?" Garret said. "Did you think you were the only one with access to intel?"

"I was hoping I had access to the right information, at least," he said, "but you guys keep hiding stuff from us."

"I'm not hiding anything," he said. "I was sent over to

talk to her. I only found out my brother was missing moments before we got on the plane that landed here."

"How long has he been missing?"

"Our intel is a little short on that," Kano said smoothly. "But we're looking at thirty-six hours, possibly forty-eight."

"Which means not very long, and, knowing you guys, maybe he's not missing at all."

"Maybe not," Garret said. "I don't know much, but I for damn sure wouldn't have made this trip on the back of another if I'd thought something wasn't behind it."

"Good point," Jonas said, as they all got out of the vehicle and walked into the lobby.

"Is Astra expecting us?" Garret asked.

"No," Jonas replied.

"So how do you know she's here?"

"I called ahead, while I was waiting for you guys."

"And don't tell me. I can guess. She still doesn't know that you're here, right?"

"I don't know if she does or not," he said. "It would be really nice of you guys to help us out though. I understand no love is lost between you and your ex-fiancée, but, if her sister can lead us to answers on your brother and Amy, that would be worth your while."

"I still want to know why you're tracking Astra, the sister," Garret said, feeling the hair on the back of his neck going up at the thought. "She's not in this industry."

"Says you," he said.

"What does that mean?"

Jonas hesitated, then shrugged. "Our intel says she's pretty high up in the government, the US government. We want to know what's going on, but nobody's talking."

"So, if you're asking us," Garret said, "then chances are

she's in one of those little secret divisions."

"That's what we're assuming because we find no sign of her on any of the websites. Also, when we Google her, we don't get anything."

"Sounds like little sister's grown up," Garret said. "You could be completely wrong though, you know?"

"It happens," Jonas said, "but not very often."

"Doesn't mean it's not happening now."

"Like we said, if it is, it is."

"Damn," he said. "I hope she isn't involved in that shit. She was a pretty nice, innocent young girl."

Just then a cold crisp voice with a hard edge cut across the lobby. "I still am, only now, I'm a woman." And she walked across, her gaze on Garret.

He stopped and stared. "Okay, little sis, you grew up."

She gave him a big hug. "We came very close to being family," she said, "but all that went by the wayside."

"I thought you would have been family by now, through my brother instead," he said.

"Your brother isn't too eager to move forward."

At that, Garret stopped and stared at her. "Seriously?"

"He said he wanted to straighten things up with you before he took any further steps in that direction."

Something inside Garret settled a little at that. "I can't imagine he loved Amy, what with the way it happened," he said. "But still, that's no excuse."

"No, it isn't," Astra said. "The only thing I can say is that I thought my sister was growing up a little bit."

"Well, there's definitely room for that," he snapped back.

She winced. "You still pining for her?"

"Hell no," he said. "She's just another life lesson, that's

all."

"Maybe so," Astra said. "But not all lessons have to be bad."

"They're never good though," he said. "So, enough of that. What are you doing here?" He motioned at the two men at his side. "Do you know these two?"

She looked at Kano, frowned, and said, "You work with Garret, don't you?"

Kano reached out a hand, introduced himself.

She nodded. "That's what I thought." She turned to look at Jonas and frowned. "You're the one who's been bugging me for information that I don't have."

Watching their interactions, Garret found nothing in her crisp assertive mannerisms even slightly reminiscent of the young girl he used to know. It was all he could do to not stare at her bemusedly.

At that point, Jonas stepped forward. "We do have a few questions."

"And I don't have any answers," she said. "Maybe now that Garret's here, we can find some though."

"What is it you think Garret can do for you?" Kano asked curiously.

Garret had to admit he was looking forward to hearing that answer as well.

She looked at Kano, then at Jonas and finally back at Garret. "He's the only one who has answers, at least according to my sister."

ASTRA WATCHED THEIR faces when she said that. She knew that Garret had already been shocked at her presence. But she wasn't the young woman he used to know. She'd grown up a lot over the last few years, becoming a little more directed, a little more focused on getting what she wanted. And what she wanted now—and in the past—was Garret, and she wanted her sister out of his life completely. But she hadn't wanted her sister to disappear.

The minute Amy had emailed, saying Gregg had gone missing and that she might have some information, Astra immediately contacted her sister, but Amy hadn't answered her phone. Neither had she given any inclination as to divulging what that information was.

As she studied the MI6 officer in front of her, Astra said, "I really don't have anything more to tell you."

"If I believed you," he said easily, "I wouldn't be here."

She glared at him.

He just smiled genuinely back at her.

"Okay, enough with the in-house fighting," Garret said.

"My sister said she had information that might help find Garret's brother, but she gave no details," Astra said coolly. "I'll forward the email to you." She pulled out her cell phone, brought it up, and showed it to Jonas. Then she said, "Give me your email." When Jonas supplied it, she forwarded the message to him. "That's it. That's all I have. Talk to Amy."

Jonas studied her for a long moment, then gave a clipped nod. "We don't have any details or even a report about Gregg being missing," he said. "But, now that we know she's involved in something to do with him, that's a whole different story."

"That's quite a leap," Astra said. "We don't know that she's involved in Gregg's disappearance."

"Maybe not," he replied, "but it's a likely deduction."

"Possibly," she admitted. Then she glanced at Garret.

"I'm sorry. She didn't give me any details, only that stupid email."

"Did you call her?"

"Yes, several times, and I got nothing." Just enough bitterness was in her voice that he was coming down on the side of believing her, and she could see it.

"That's why I flew over," she said. "I was actually in France for a conference at the time."

"Are you in the government? Like, high up?"

She gave a bitter laugh. "No," she said. "I used to be." She looked at Jonas. "Your intel's a little outdated."

He shrugged.

"I now work for a private security company," she said.

"Please tell me it's not Kingdom Securities," Garret said.

She smiled. "No, it's not them, and it's not Bullard's team either, or you would know."

He nodded slowly. "Not too many other big players. Legendary Security out of Texas being the other."

"Different kind of intelligence," she said. "I'm working with an international cybersecurity company."

"Okay," he said. "So you know about my brother being missing—your sister too—but have you done anything to find them?"

"Outside of contacting you?"

"Yes."

"Not a whole lot," she said. "I've sent out some feelers, but I don't have any answers at this time." She looked back at Jonas. "So, as I said, I really don't have anything more to offer you." Then, adding an unexpected twist to the conversation, she asked Jonas a question of her own. "Do you have anything to offer me?"

He shook his head. "No, we don't."

She nodded., "In that case, I guess you can leave then, right?"

"I guess so," he said, frowning. He turned to the other two men and said, "I can give you a ride."

"No need," Garret said. "We'll be fine."

Jonas nodded and turned to leave. After a few steps, he stopped and did a half turn, looking back at Garret and Kano. "You will keep me apprised of your comings and goings, correct?"

"Of course," he said. "I'm here to find my brother."

"See that you stay in touch," Jonas replied, and, with that, he walked out.

Astra turned to Garret. "Do you want to go to the coffee shop or up to my room to talk?"

"Upstairs," he said immediately. "We also need to get our own lodging taken care of."

Kano nudged him gently. "I'll go ahead and give Charles a call," he said, already on his phone.

"What room are you in?" Garret asked, as he turned to Astra.

"Room 212," she replied, then led the way to the stairs.

Kano nodded to Garret, still on the phone, indicating he would join them soon.

Astra walked up one flight of stairs, then turned to the left. Garret followed behind her. "Are you doing okay?" Astra asked Garret.

"It's been a rough few weeks," he replied.

She shot him a glance. "I heard about the plane crash. Are you really okay? The reports varied wildly from one side to the other. I didn't know what to believe."

"I'm sure the intel was all over the place. I'm fine now though. A few extra metal pieces, some residual headaches, but I'm back to work." He shrugged, as little could be done now but give his body time to heal. Too bad the bad blood between his brother, Amy, and Garret couldn't heal quite so easily. He and his brother had barely spoken in the last three years. Same for Amy. "I wondered why my brother wasn't there when I came out of the coma."

"I'm thinking he didn't know," she said. "And even Amy seemed shocked, when I mentioned the accident."

"Yeah, but that would imply that Gregg was in trouble even then."

"It hasn't been that long, has it?"

"Four weeks," he said.

"Should you even be back to duty?"

"Good luck to anyone trying to tell me not to be," he said, his voice hard.

She nodded. "Understood."

"How are your parents?"

"Both are deceased," she said, her tone short. "It's just Amy and me now."

"I'm sorry," he said.

"We've never been close as a family, but, after her split from you, there was a rift between all of us," she said, with a shrug.

"Understood," he said. "You weren't exactly happy about what she did, as I recall."

"No, I wasn't," she said. "I've tried to talk to your brother about it a couple times, but he won't discuss it. He always has this kind of haunted look on his face."

"That sort of explains it," Garret said, with a smile.

"I think Amy took him by surprise."

"Yeah, she has that effect on people," he said.

"In all fairness to the two of them, I honestly think what

they have is something that they may make work." He looked at her in surprise, as she shrugged. "I know. I wasn't happy about how they started their relationship without your knowledge, but, now that I see them together, I think it's a better match than the two of you were."

"No doubt," he said. "No way I want to be married to somebody I can't trust."

"That always meant a lot to you, didn't it?" she said, as she unlocked the door.

He walked in behind her, as she tossed her purse and keys on the small counter, then headed to the small coffeemaker and set it up for a pot. She watched him as he surveyed the room. He was tall, dark-haired, lean, and looking a little stressed from everything he'd been going through. His color was a little pale, but, all in all, he looked almost back to full strength.

His gaze suddenly pierced through her. "So, do I pass muster?"

She nodded. "Sorry. I was just checking to see how physically exhausted you were. That was a major accident."

"Well, I can tell you one thing. Anger, outrage, and the need for revenge are great motivators," he said. "I'll make it through."

"I have no doubt about that," she said, with a half smile. "No doubt at all."

CHAPTER 2

A STRA KNEW SHE shouldn't say anything, but she'd never been any good at staying quiet. "That also doesn't mean you should be putting yourself into more danger than you need to be."

"And I won't," Garret said, his tone cool. Then got to the point. "So you obviously wanted me alone. What is it you wanted to say?" She hesitated, and he shook his head. "I don't have time for games here, Astra."

"None of us do," she said. "It's my sister too."

"Got it. We're both in a position of having to look for our cheating siblings. Siblings that we're currently on the outs with."

She gave a bitter laugh. "You could say that," she said. "What I don't know is what we're supposed to do about it?"

"All that drama aside," he said, "we still have to figure out what's going on and try to help them."

"I don't even know where to start," she said, raising her hands in the air.

"Where has Amy been living?"

"In Belgium was the last I knew," she said, "but she was looking to relocate. I don't know where. But the last time I actually saw her, she was in Paris."

"So maybe we need to go there," he murmured.

"No, that was a few years ago. I think she left Belgium

because of some danger. I just don't know what or why. She wouldn't tell me," she said.

"Listen, Astra. I get that you're frustrated, and God knows your sister has an exceptional ability to do that to both of us. But, if she came from Belgium, then chances are that's where we need to start our investigation."

She frowned at him. "I don't work in quite the same field as you, but I wanted to start tracking her online."

"What you mean is that you've already started, right?" he said, studying her carefully.

She smiled. "You know me so well."

"In many ways I do," he said. "For a while there, it seemed like I was spending more time with you than with Amy."

"I know," she answered, trying to keep her feelings out of her expression. "So why the hell did you even keep waiting around for my sister?"

"I don't know. I should have seen what she was like from the beginning."

"What I think you should have seen was the attraction between Amy and your brother and the fact that they were hiding something," she said.

"Yeah, I know, but it's hard to see that kind of stuff when you're locked inside your own feelings," he said. "I honestly didn't see it." Realization dawned on his face. "Are you saying that you did?"

She nodded. "I did."

"Did you think that maybe you should have said something to me?"

"Are you kidding? Nobody could tell you anything," she said in exasperation. "Especially me."

He burst out with a laugh. "Well, that hasn't changed.

I'm still pretty bull-headed."

"Surprise, surprise," she murmured.

He just looked at her, as she shrugged. Then came a knock on the door. "I imagine it's Kano."

At that, the knock continued with an odd pattern to it.

Garret nodded and said, "Definitely Kano." He walked over, opened the door, and smiled when he saw his buddy.

"Good thing you're still around," Kano said. "I had visions of you getting a hot lead and taking off on me."

"Not yet, but we need to get some intel pretty quickly."

"It's possible we could get some from Jonas," Kano said, "and Charles is expecting us tonight."

"Good, at least we have that locked down." Looking at Astra, he said, "So, outside of Belgium, what do you have to offer?"

"I'm not even sure Belgium has anything to offer," she said. "All I can tell you is that none of my sister's credit cards have been used in the last twenty-four hours and neither has her cell phone." Hesitating, she finally added reluctantly. "Your brother's phone hasn't been used either."

"You tracked it?"

She nodded. "That was the easy part. After that, it gets much harder."

"That's true," he said.

GARRET DIDN'T KNOW what to make of Astra at this point. She was so different, and it was hard to see the young girl he recognized from before, yet she came out in little glimpses. He took a deep breath. "Why do I feel like you're holding something back?"

She hesitated and then nodded. "Part of the reason for

Amy moving from Belgium to London was that she'd given your brother an ultimatum."

"Why?"

She sighed, then shrugged. "Amy's pregnant."

That news was like a punch to his gut. "Jesus," he said. "Did my brother know?"

"I don't know if she told him or not. What I do know is that she wanted a different life, and it was important to her."

"So it's my brother's child?"

"It's your niece or nephew, yes," she confirmed.

He stared off in the distance, still getting his mind wrapped around it.

"So, whatever feelings you may still have for her," she said, "you probably need to walk away from them completely."

He waved a hand at her. "I walked away a long time ago."

"But I still get the feeling that you're emotionally affected."

"Not by her but by her deception, her affair with my brother," he said. "However, for my brother, a pregnancy would be a big deal."

"Any reason why?"

"He's always said he didn't plan to be a father," Garret murmured.

"Plans change when the facts hit the fan," she said, her voice cool. "I wouldn't think he'd be somebody to ditch his responsibilities though."

"Oh, I don't think he would either," he said. "I'm not sure that we know what's going on in their personal life, outside of the fact that a big change is happening."

"Exactly," she agreed.

"And, if my brother is missing and if it's something suspicious, it would make sense that she would reach out to me through my team," he said.

"Why not the cops?"

"Because of the type of work my brother does, which is very similar to what I do for Bullard—meaning we avoid local law enforcement at all costs and only communicate with the big agencies as a courtesy. Also we heard some suspicion or a theory that he might have had something to do with the plane crash."

At that, Astra looked at him in shock. "The plane crash you were in?"

He shrugged. "I wouldn't have thought my brother hated me that much, but honestly I don't know. Maybe he does."

"I would say that he did not, but you're right. We don't know because we haven't seen them in years," she said heavily. "I do talk to Amy at times, but only because she's called me to complain. And you have to take her words with a grain of salt."

Garret nearly growled.

Astra nodded. "People change, but I would hope not to that extent."

"You and me both," he said, with a hard look.

She nodded and said quietly, "I get that you don't like hearing about any of this going on between Amy and Gregg, but it's still totally possible that Gregg had nothing to do with it. I'd like to believe he's better than that. Especially as I heard he wanted to reconcile with you."

Garret was still dealing with the shock of thinking of his brother as a father. Gregg was younger, a little wilder, and didn't have quite the reasoning ability that Garret had. But they'd always been close—until Amy came between them. And, for that, he would always hold Amy off to the side because she'd been the thorn that festered.

Kano, quietly listening from the corner, joined the conversation. "That also explains why she may have disappeared now," Kano interjected.

"How so?" Garret asked.

"Hormones. Pregnancy sets off a storm of hormones, and she may well be seeing things that aren't there," he said, "or interpreting them differently that she would otherwise. Or seeing her life as it is and wanting more. Needing maybe time alone to think."

Astra winced at that. "I get that whole raging-hormones thing with a pregnancy," she said, "and I know my sister is on the border of being neurotic in many ways already. But I would hope that she's erring on the side of safety, for the baby if not for herself."

Garret agreed. "I would say she's definitely protecting the safety of the baby, no doubt about it. Probably in a manner that's way over-the-top, knowing her." That statement prompted a snicker out of Astra. "Now it's a matter of figuring out how we find them," Garret said.

"Well, I'm doing what I can do," she said. "But I fear I'm in way over my head. My question is, what will you do?"

"Get them back," Garret said. "Let's just hope we can do it before something bad happens."

CHAPTER 3

O N THE HEELS of that statement, chaos reigned. Garret's phone went off, and so did Kano's. Astra went over to the counter and picked up her coffee cup, then walked to the window. She'd rented this hotel room because it was the same hotel her sister had been in. She hadn't been allowed access to her sister's room, and, as far as she knew, the police had been in, searched, and gone. She had yet to provide that room number to Garret though.

As soon as they were off the phone, she said, "My sister was staying here, also on the second floor."

"You and I'll head there now. Kano will stay here. Also I've got the team searching for whatever they can turn up, and I've contacted Charles."

"Who is this Charles?" she asked, as they walked to the door.

"Somebody in town who works in our field."

"Good for him."

"No, he should have retired a long time ago. In fact, he has one of those jobs that you just never retire from." He walked to the door, waiting for her to join him, then he shut it, as he walked out into the hallway with her.

"What about Kano?"

"Kano's on his own mission to get information. We'll pull as many threads as we can to get people on board."

"Do you have a team?"

"A lot of team members," he said, with a nod. "And we're running with other teams as well."

She wasn't quite sure what that meant but was willing to accept any help coming their way.

"Had Amy been working?"

"No, not in the last few weeks. She'd been doing contract work for art graphics. Websites, logos, branding, things like that. But, since she found out she was pregnant, things kind of went to pot for her."

"Again, those emotions boiling over," he murmured.

"And again, not necessarily all that there is to this," she said. "I get that she's not your favorite person at the moment. Yet, whatever is happening, she needs help."

"I get it and would hope that you still know me better than that," he said. "But the bottom line is that definitely some aspect of her pregnancy is involved here, no matter what else is going on. Being pregnant makes everything different for her."

"There's also a chance that she's taken off because she felt she was in danger."

"But you have no way to contact her?"

"I've tried every way I know," she said. "Social media, text, cell phone, old phone numbers, messages with friends. Everything I can think of, but nothing's turned up so far."

"How was your relationship lately? Is she likely to respond?"

"I would have thought so, yes," she said, but again she shrugged.

"But?"

"She knew that I didn't approve of her getting pregnant and having his baby."

"Why not?" he said, almost offended at the suggestion that something was wrong with his brother.

"Because she wanted desperately for her baby to have a father who would be home, and, with all his traveling, in no way does Gregg fit that model."

"No," Garret said. "He doesn't."

"Why are you getting all defensive about it anyway?" she asked, looking at him sideways. "Like I insulted him or something. Look at you. How could you possibly believe he would have anything to do with your accident?" she asked. "Do you really think he'd cause a plane crash over the middle of the ocean?"

"Only because of what Amy said. That she had information and thought he was involved somehow."

"That came from her? That doesn't add up at all. I just don't get it. She never said anything about that to me," she said, sounding upset.

"Unless …" Garret said, speaking slowly, thinking as he spoke. "Unless she thought that would somehow guarantee that I would come over here and talk to her. She is the last person I want anything to do with, and she knows it."

"That actually makes sense," Astra murmured. "She would try whatever she could to make you come and help look for him."

"But then she bails and takes off, so we're not even sure what the score is right now," he said, frowning.

"*If* she took off," she said. "What if she was taken instead?"

He rolled his eyes at that. "Okay, for the moment, we'll assume that something has happened to both of them. Which makes sense, but I'd just as soon have some proof before we head down that rabbit hole."

"What if there isn't any proof?"

"Then we're in trouble," he said. "It's pretty hard to move forward, if you don't know what the hell you are supposed to do next."

"I know," she said, and she did. "It's just so damn frustrating and frightening. We've never been all that close, but I wouldn't wish this on my worst enemy, much less my sister. I know the pregnancy was weighing on her terribly. Wherever she is, she's got to be petrified."

"I'm sure she is," he said gently. "And, Astra, despite my history with your sister, I'll do whatever I can, for both of them."

"I know that," she said, with a nod. "Your own sense of honor won't let you do anything else."

"Sometimes I think that damn sense of honor is a joke," he murmured.

"Why is that?" she asked.

"Because it's something I can't get away from. Other people aren't handicapped by that same set of standards."

She knew he was referring, once again, to his brother and her sister having an illicit affair. "The only thing I can say is that, together, they saw something that they really wanted."

"Yeah, most people break up first or at least tell you what's going on. You don't have to find out the hard way, after the fact."

She winced at that because he had found out in the worst possible way. Personally, when they had come out of a bedroom, obviously having just had sex. "I'm sorry about that," she murmured.

"It's not your fault," he said. "Honestly I'd like to think that I've gotten over it, but apparently I'm still bitter."

"You think?" she said and laughed. "I think that you just haven't replaced her yet, and that's the problem."

"I would never replace her," he said. "I don't replace something that's broken or bad. Instead I find something way better."

She looked at him with surprise and then shrugged. "I can see that's how you would look at it, and I'm sorry my sister failed in that department."

"Whatever," he said. "Enough of that." They were outside her sister's hotel room now. "Did you ask the hotel to get in early on?"

"I did and was refused. I'm sure it was searched and all, but I never heard anything about it."

He nodded. "Give me just a second."

When she stepped back, she whispered, "Are you trying to break in?" Turning, she looked toward the elevator. "What if somebody sees you?" Turning back, he was already inside. She made a startled sound and stepped forward. "How did you do that so fast?"

"It's what I do," he said gently.

She nodded. "I get that, but—"

"No buts," he said, as he gestured for her to come inside. She walked in behind him, and he closed the door.

"It doesn't look like it's been disturbed," she said.

"I presume the police know about this because Jonas contacted me about it too. They should have put a lock on the room, so nobody could get in."

"Nobody other than you, you mean?"

"Well, yeah," he said, without making any excuses for it.

She always liked that about him. He knew where he was going, what he was doing, and how he would get there. Her sister, who had always been a follower, just seemed to be dragged along in his wake. Astra always wondered what the odd pairing was between them, but, as they had been together for well over a year, and then he'd actually proposed, she'd been stunned when her sister had said yes, but again she was a follower. The only time she had really broken that habit was when she'd had the affair with Gregg. And that had been enough to make Astra sit up and take note of Gregg because that was so uncharacteristic for her sister. Astra realized it must have taken a lot for Amy to do something so unusual like that.

Anytime somebody's behavior went off the wall, it was important to find out what the catalyst was. In this case, Astra had put it down to being something her sister really wanted. A baby, which brought up all kinds of other stuff. But, in Astra's world, it was all good because of all the things that Astra had wanted in her life, one had always been Garret.

When she'd first met him, she'd been struck by the love bug. And it never disappeared. When Amy and Garret had broken up, Astra had been ecstatic, yet sympathetic, and had just bided her time. To think that it could possibly be the right time now was amazing, and yet the fact that he was still so angry and hurt made Astra very aware of just how much damage her sister's actions had done.

Somehow Astra had to get him to see that it really wasn't just about her sister and her actions as much as it was a broken trust with her and his brother. Working in cybersecurity had afforded Astra the opportunity to learn in some detail why people betrayed each other. It usually boiled down to some fairly common basic elements, but they were always most painful for the person who never saw it coming.

That's what this was, all over again. Garret was always

very strict about honor and justice and believing in each other and loyalty. That's why he made such a great team player because he trusted the rest of his team, and he always had everybody's back. Yet the type of work he did was also very much a loner's game, but, when he needed help, he had people to call on, and that's what she presumed he was up to right now. Because, if ever they needed help, it was to get these two people back again.

The fact that her sister was pregnant had Astra twisted up inside. She didn't want anything to happen to her family. It was just the two of them left in this world, and to think that her sister was embarking on that journey perhaps alone, in such difficult times, was something Astra didn't want to think about. She could only hope that this would all come to a good ending. The only way to do that was to give Garret as much help as she could.

As she walked around her sister's hotel room, she said, "It's almost like she was hardly here."

"It's a hotel room," he murmured. "How much do people actually put their stamp on it?"

"My sister is messy, if you recall," she said. "Everything here has been neatly packed up. As if she was barely here, or she never had a chance to unpack, or she was already packing to leave."

He turned to look at her and said, "How do you know that she didn't actually just pack up and leave?"

"I don't know that," she said. "I just know she hasn't responded to any communication from me, and she's obviously not here, nor has she been here in a while."

He nodded. "Definitely something suspicious is going on." He did a thorough search of the hotel room and then looked at the suitcase and said, "I need to check that over."

"Go for it," she said. "She's hardly here to argue."

"And yet somehow I hear her voice screaming at me in the background."

She laughed at that. "It's funny, the things we remember."

"Not really," he said. "The only thing I remember is the betrayal."

"Because that's where you were hurt the most," she said, with a nod. He looked at her and frowned. "No, I'm not psychoanalyzing you," she said, with a wave of her hand. "But it makes sense when you think about it."

"And what if I don't want to think about it?" he said. "Your sister is not somebody I ever really want to think about."

"And yet this doesn't give us much chance to do anything other than think about her."

He shrugged. "Potentially," he said, unwilling to buckle.

She smiled and said, "You have to gamble sometimes."

"I'm not a gambler."

"I know," she said, "but sometimes you have to take people on faith. You have to take a gamble on them."

"Can't say I'll do that again. I did that with your sister. The only way to deal with her is with an attack plan and placing the opening gambit."

She winced at that. "Not everybody is my sister," she said, with asperity.

"Maybe not, but, once I found out that there were people like your sister," he said, "you can bet that I pulled back on the trust factor."

"Got it," she said, "and again, not everybody is my sister."

"No, but enough are out there," he said, "that I really

don't want to have anything to do with her, or him for that matter, ever again."

She groaned. "You'll have to get over that," she snapped.

"And why is that?" he asked.

"Because that attitude won't serve you very well for long."

"I don't know," he said. "It's served me quite well so far."

"You're just bitter."

"Maybe so, "he said, "but that's life."

"It's only life if you don't want to change."

He shot her hard look. "Did you have a reason for this crazy conversation?"

"No, I just thought it would be important to share it with you," she said, with a shrug. "Did you see anything, in my sister's stuff?"

"No," he said. "Nothing's here. Her purse is gone. There's nothing personal—no paperwork, no wallet, nothing like that."

"Makes sense," she said.

"How does it make sense?"

"She'd take her purse, if she made a fast run out of here," she said. "Then obviously something could be going on."

"Maybe, but it's also possible that she was kidnapped from this room, and they snatched her purse too. Or she was out shopping and was taken off the street." He looked up and frowned, adding, "Because I found no car keys, no hotel keys either."

"Oh." She looked around and said, "No, you're right. But then those would be in her purse, right?"

"Potentially."

GARRET PULLED OUT his phone and called Jonas. "You want to help? Check video feeds of people leaving around the hotel. Amy's purse isn't here. I found no hotel key to get in and out. If she's been snatched outside, there should be video of it somewhere."

"Will do." And, with that, he hung up.

"That was fast," she said.

"No need to prolong it. Either somebody can find her face out there on the cameras or not."

"Do you think it's possible that she was snatched outside?"

"That makes the most sense to me, yes. Inside, they have to find a way to get her out of here. Outside, she's already there and could quickly be moved into a vehicle. But unless somebody is actually looking for something like that, nobody'll go through those hours on a camera feed to find it."

"How can they even do that anyway?"

"Facial recognition software," he said. "Even then, it's hit or miss. Takes a lot of time, so you need a lot of computer power to spare to do it."

"You have somebody to do that?"

"I just tagged MI6," he said. "She's gone missing on their watch, after all."

"Well, they were hardly watching her," she murmured.

"Don't you worry," he said. "If they've been watching for my brother, they've been watching for her."

"Shit," she said. "Is there a chance that this whole thing is a government-run deal?"

He stopped, looked at her, and said, "Better not be. You haven't seen me angry, but, if I find out Jonas's involved in this—"

"The only reason for that would be ... what?"

"Oh, if they are looking for my brother and have no way to find him."

"But wouldn't they contact you about that?"

"Well, guess who picked us up at the airport? You saw him yourself."

"That still doesn't make any sense."

"They work in mysterious ways," he murmured. "The only reason they'd be interested in my brother is if they think he has something to do with something else." He pulled out his phone, called Jonas, and said, "Did you take her?"

On the other end, Jonas squawked, "What?"

"Did you take Amy? Hoping that she'd lead you to my brother maybe?"

"No," Jonas said, his tone forceful and believable. "We didn't take her."

"Good thing," he said. "You know I'd have your heart, if you did."

"Thanks so much for the trust," Jonas snapped.

"Just checking." He hung up his phone, then turned and looked at her. "Nope, they don't have her."

"And you trust him?"

"Remember that part about not trusting anybody?"

"But you trust your team?"

"Give it a rest, will you?" he said, suddenly tired. "I trust those I trust, but, once that trust is broken, it's hard to get it back."

"Good point," she murmured, as they walked toward the door. "Anything else to be looked at in here?"

"No," he said. Just then a knock came on the door. He watched, as she froze instantly. He lifted his finger to his lips, walked to the door to the adjoining hotel room, and motioned for her to come toward him. She quickly joined him, as she heard a card key swiping in the lock at the same moment that Garret got the connecting door unlocked and pulled her inside.

"You don't know who it is," she whispered. "Why are we running away?"

"Last time I looked, we didn't have permission to be there," he said. "Besides, this way we get to know who else is coming in."

Just then she heard a voice on the other side of the connecting door.

"I thought you said you saw them come in here?"

"I thought I did too," he said, "but now I don't know."

"There isn't any room for 'I don't know.' We have to keep an eye on anybody that's in this room."

"I still don't think she would know anything."

"She buggered off on us while we were trying to keep track of her, so we have to assume she knows something," one man said.

At that, Garret stepped out of the adjoining room and said, "Hello, gentlemen. Were you looking for me?"

CHAPTER 4

ASTRA WATCHED THROUGH the crack, as the two men stared at him in shock. They were obviously not hotel employees.

"Who are you?" one of the men asked rudely.

She heard the crispness in Garret's voice as he spoke. "Well, obviously, if I'm part of the other suite, I'm looking for the woman who's in here. She's with my party."

"Sure," the one guy said, with a sneer.

Then, in a move so smooth and practiced, she was almost shocked when Garret's right hand smacked the guy on the side of the head with a light punch.

"Don't talk about her that like that," he said.

The guy stepped back. "What the fuck?"

"I said, what do you know about her, and why are you watching her room?"

"You don't know anything about me," the one guy said. "I don't have to stay here and talk to you." And, with that, he strode to the door and flung it open, only to see Kano standing there, a grim smile on his face. He stepped in, pushing the two men back into the room.

"Now you are the guys we want to talk to," Garret said. "So talk. What do you know about her disappearance?"

"We don't know anything. We were just supposed to keep an eye on the room, and I saw these two go in, so I told my boss," the one man said, as he was still nursing his sore cheek. "And I didn't need to get punched in the face for it."

"Well, you're the one who's tracking a single woman," Astra said angrily, coming into the room. "And why is that again?"

The men looked at her, looked at Garret, then looked back to Kano and said, "We don't have to talk to anybody."

"Well, you don't have to," Garret replied, and, with that, pulled out his phone and said, "You can talk to MI6 instead." At that, the two men froze. "I thought so," he said, as he hit Jonas's number and said, "Jonas, I'm sending you photos of the two men, watching Amy's room. We've got them pinned inside her room right now."

"Don't kill them," Jonas's voice came through the phone, sharp and crisp.

The two men stared at the phone in shock.

"I'll try not to," he said, "but you don't like it when we cause damage. Isn't that what you said when you picked us up at the airport? That we always cause damage?"

"Yeah, and, in this case, I suspect you're about to cause damage to a hotel room and several people. Well, if they need to be damaged, then I guess I'm okay with it."

"You know how I feel about assholes."

"Yes, I do," he said. "I'm on my way."

"Better get here fast." He hung up the phone, looked at the two intruders, and asked, "You want to talk to us, or you want to talk to MI6?"

"We don't want anything to do with MI6," one man said, looking at the other. "We're actually from Scotland."

"You don't have accents," she said, stepping up beside Garret. "I don't believe you. What do you have to do with my sister? Did you have anything to do with her disappearance?"

The first man raised his hands, palms up. "No, we were hired to keep an eye on the apartment and to see who came to look after her, to look in on her, I mean."

"It's a hotel room, not an apartment, dumbass," Garret said. "So you better get things straight here. Because we'll check it out, and, if you're lying, I will personally take you apart."

"Look. We were hired to keep a watch on this place. That's it. It was my watch, when you guys showed up. I reported seeing you go in. That's all there is to it."

"And you told who?" Kano asked, coming around to study the two men, as he sent pictures to his team and to Jonas.

"The guy who hired us," he answered. Then quickly added, "And I don't know anything about him. I get a phone call. I get a deposit of money in my account, half up front, half when the job's done. Other than that, I can't tell you anything."

"Not sure I believe you," he said. "What's the number?"

He hesitated and immediately Kano came and searched him. He pulled out his wallet, cell phone, and, with a quick search, found a piece on his ankle. He pulled that out and whistled. "Jonas will love this."

"No, he won't," Garret said, "he won't love it at all."

"But that's all right. He needed a reason to come and get you guys anyway." Kano sent a picture of the handgun to Jonas, and then they went through the guy's wallet.

"Hey, you don't need to do that."

"What I see is that you don't have enough to buy yourself some chips at the corner store," he said. "So maybe you better try that line again."

"It's the truth," he said. "I don't have any money. That's why I'm even doing this, and it's all bullshit."

Kano checked out the guy's name. "Funny, you got IDs in here but two different names."

"So what?" he said. "That's just the life I live."

"Got it," he said. "It kind of sucks though, huh? You never really know which name to answer to."

"Fuck off," he said. "You guys ain't nobody to talk."

As they waited and watched, now with the weapon in Kano's hand, they searched the second man. "One set of ID, a little more money than you, but not much. Both of you stooges are broke."

"That's the reason we're doing this," the second man said, in a quiet voice. "And we really just want to get the hell out of here."

"If you don't offer up something useful," Garret said, "then we can't let you go."

"What do you want?"

"The guy who hired you," Astra said. "Are you that stupid?" Both men just glared at her. "Listen, assholes. She's my sister, and I want her back, now."

"I'm sure you do, but we don't know anything about her disappearance."

"Well, presumably the guys who took her are the ones wanting to keep track of who comes here," Garret said. "So you need to tell us who that is, before I even think about letting you go."

"You don't understand. We'll never get any more work, if we do that."

"Well, he won't be hiring you anymore anyway, so you'll have the same problem either way. We'll find this guy no matter what. It's just a matter of whether we find him sooner or later."

"But, if he finds out we snitched on him, it won't be good for us," he said.

"It's already ugly," Garret said, "because we'll make sure your faces hit the news today, and they're already writing you off as people who may have turned on them."

"We're not snitches!"

"But they don't know that, do they?" Garret said.

Kano looked at the men. "You said you're broke, right? A little money must go a long way then, huh?"

"So you'll pay us then?" asked the second man, eyeing him. "We might do a deal then."

The first man hit him. "Look, Sonny. We'll get in a shit ton of trouble this way."

"We're already in a shit ton of trouble," Sonny said, "just in case you didn't get the memo."

The first man looked directly at his buddy. "We'll never get more work after this. You know that. Not with them anyway."

"Not too many choices for us," Sonny said.

"I know, but this isn't going well." With a long exhale, he turned to Garret. "How much?"

"You tell me," he said, with a sigh. "Everybody's got a price. What's yours?"

"One thousand pounds," he said instantly.

"Interesting figure," he said. "And you answered pretty quick. Why?"

"That's what we were supposed to get for this job, which we won't get now, thanks to you."

"That's a decent amount for watching a hotel room. Especially the room of a woman nobody has anything to do with," Garret said.

"A thousand pounds between the two of you isn't a hell of a lot of money either. Particularly if you've already been given half of it up front," Kano said.

"A thousand pounds each and we walk," the first man said.

Garret laughed at him. "Didn't take very long to find your price, did it?"

At that, a hard knock came at the door. Kano walked over and let Jonas in. "They're trying to sell the information they have for one thousand pounds," he said. "Each."

"Wow, that's almost insulting."

"It is, but these guys are lowlifes. All we can hope to get is the next rung up the ladder."

"Which sucks because we really need several rungs up the ladder."

"They don't know anything," she said. "They're just losers anyway."

"We know enough," Sonny said.

"Do you?" she said, with another sneer. "Prove it. Why should anybody give you anything anyway? You should just get a life sentence for being two-bit losers."

"Hardly," the first guy said, getting into it. "You're the one who's a loser."

She rolled her eyes at that.

Garret reached out, grabbed him by the scruff of the neck, and said, "You have anything to say or not?"

"Only if I get one thousand pounds," he said.

Garret shoved him over to Jonas. "Personally I would just deep-six them. Don't even bother about a trial or anything. Nobody'll miss these punks anyway."

"You can't do that," the second man said.

"Sure we can, … Sonny. You don't have anything useful

to offer. So, as far as we're concerned, you're nothing but cheats. You've already turned on your boss, so we couldn't trust anything we got from you anyway," he said, with a sneer.

The man studied him for a long moment. "We got something good," he said.

"Don't do it," the other guy said.

"We don't really have a whole lot of choice," he said. "Think about it. We got to get out of this."

"It doesn't matter if we get out or not. We'll still be gone."

"Which is why we need to get what we can," he said. He looked at Jonas. "You MI6?"

"Yes," he said.

"In that case," he said. "We just want freedom."

"Not sure that freedom is something you can have," he said.

"We have rung number one and rung number two," he said, looking back at Garret. "We don't know who is above them."

"So, who's the first one?" he asked, and the man gave up the guy's name easily enough.

"His name is Larry. He runs a bunch of cons here in town."

"Larry Overhaul?" Jonas asked.

They looked at him and nodded.

"He does a lot of smuggling from the mainland over here, doesn't he?"

"Yeah."

Jonas looked back at Garret. "That checks out."

"Sure, but that's minor stuff. Nobody's talking about why my sister's gone missing," Astra said. "Without something hard, these guys shouldn't get squat."

"She has information they want," he said.

"Do they have her?" she asked.

"I don't think so. They tried to snag her, and she ran."

"Well, that would be good," Astra murmured, feeling a sense of relief take over. Her sister was flighty, but, since the pregnancy, Amy had changed in many ways, and one of the things that she'd been adamant about was that she needed to leave. And she had, so maybe it was for the best. "So maybe she's not missing then. Maybe she just took off on her own?" She faced Garret with a frown.

"Maybe. They want to know where she is though," the second man said. "They won't stop until they find her."

"What is this information she has that they are after?" Kano asked.

"Kingdom Securities."

"What about them?" Garret said, glaring directly at him. "What about Kingdom?"

"Some question of loyalty there."

"What does it matter to them?"

"They didn't get paid for something," he said. "A big job, somebody was supposed to be involved, and they didn't get paid."

"So?"

"There's some discrepancy as to who in Kingdom hired them."

"Does this have to do with the flight?" Garret asked.

"Well, they hired the subcontractors and had to pay that out. But it was a big, big plan that didn't come to fruition, and they didn't get paid."

"Well, if they failed at the job, why would they get paid?"

"They told him there was a slim chance of success, so they wanted payment regardless."

"Let me get this straight," Garret said. "You think they got hired by somebody within Kingdom who didn't have the backing of the company?"

"Yeah. Like a private deal."

"And who was it that set up this private deal?"

"That's why they wanted her."

"Why?" Garret said. "I want to hear it. Why?"

"Because it was her boyfriend, and a lot of money is involved. They think she has the money or at least access to it. And, if not to the money, they think she can lead them to him. Gregg. His name is Gregg."

THE TWO MEN were gone. Jonas had taken them away, and Garret was back in Astra's room, pacing the floor.

"You don't have to believe him," she said.

"I don't believe him," he said. "I know Amy came between my brother and me, but I'd like to think me and my brother had a whole lot more between us than her."

"Do you think she could have poisoned the relationship that much?"

"I would like to think not," he said, but his tone was cold, cutting. The last thing he wanted right now was to analyze his brother's relationship with Amy. It was bad enough that Garret was even here, having to deal with Gregg's disappearance. And that Gregg's girlfriend, and apparently the mother of his child, had obviously booked it and was hiding out somewhere. But to think that his brother actually had a hand in the plane crash that nearly killed Garret, that was taking things farther than Garret was comfortable with. He spun around and stared at Kano. "There has to be another explanation."

"There will be," he said comfortably. And that was one of the great things about Kano. He was always there to be on your side. If they found out that it would be something uglier than Garret wanted to look at right now, they would both deal with it later.

Garret took a long slow deep breath. "Right." He spun and looked at Astra. "Think about places that she could have gone," he said. "Where would she go, if she's hiding out because she's terrified?"

"I've been trying to figure that out," she said, feeling bewildered. "I just don't know where she would go."

"Do you have any other property? Or does she? Did your parents have any property?"

"Oh, crap," she said, staring at him in surprise. "Remember the cabin? You guys went there, and I met you there that one day. Remember?"

He nodded slowly. "Yes. What about it?"

"She used to always go there, when she was upset. We both did. It gave us time to think."

"Which is why she was there then, after I proposed, but I thought it was her favorite place."

She gave him a sad smile. "No, that's where she used to go to make the major decisions in her life."

"That's where she told me that she would marry me," he said, frowning.

"I know," she said. "I presume she was struggling with her answer because that's where she goes when she has those kinds of troubles."

"How far away is it?" Kano asked.

"About an hour, hour and a half or so from here," she

said. "Up the coast."

"Well, let's go then," Kano said. "Because I'd put money down on this one." When they didn't jump up, he looked at Garret on the left and Astra on the right, from one to the other. "So, have you got any other ideas where she could be?"

"No," she said slowly. "That would be my bad."

"Then let's go." At that, the three of them jumped up and headed downstairs.

"Wait. We don't have a car," she said.

"Yeah, we do," Kano replied. "It'll be here in a minute."

"Whose is it?"

"Charles's," he said. "I'll have to remember to thank him. So far, we haven't even seen him yet on this trip, but some trips are like that."

"Unfortunately a lot of our trips are like that," Garret said. He looked at Astra, who was standing outside, her hands in her pockets, her purse slung over her shoulder, and her long blond hair blowing back in the breeze. She was stunning. How come he hadn't noticed that before? Well, he had, but it hadn't been kosher at the time. She was his girlfriend's little sister, after all, so he'd always kept the looking to a minimum. But no need to do that any longer, and, man, she was gorgeous.

She turned and looked at him, noticed the look in his eyes and then frowned. "What are you looking at?"

"A beautiful woman," he said, and she frowned even more. "Still don't know how to take a compliment, huh?"

"Haven't received very many of them in my lifetime," she said. "Not enough to get comfortable with it anyway."

Kano looked at them, frowning, as he picked up on the conversation, his gaze going from one to the other. Then he gave half a headshake and turned away.

She looked at him. "What was that look for?"

"Nothing," he said. "I just see the cycle happening again. It's bloody amazing."

"If you say so," she said, obviously not understanding.

But Garret understood. He gave a hard frown in Kano's direction. "Hardly the same thing."

"Exactly the same thing, Garret," he snapped. "Just don't let it infect me, will you."

At that, Garret laughed. "Well, buddy, if I'm infected, you're already exposed."

"Better not be," he snapped. "I don't need that shit in my life right now."

"Nobody ever needs it when it comes," Garret said. "You have to be ready, just in case though."

"Hell no, I don't. You can go play that game all you want, but I don't have to."

"Says you," he said. "Anyway, it's a minor point."

"Says you."

Just then a car pulled up in front. The driver got out, walked around, and handed Kano the keys. "Please bring this one back in one piece, if you can."

Kano laughed. "Always," he said. "If I can, anyway."

"Says you," the man quipped, as he walked down the street and disappeared.

"Who was that?" she asked.

"Somebody I've met a time or two," Kano said, with a big grin. "Jump in. We've got places to go." With that, they all climbed in and hit the road.

CHAPTER 5

A STRA DIDN'T WANT to admit, even to herself, how uncomfortable Garret's comment about her appearance made her feel. It's what she had always wanted, but, in this instance, and in these surroundings, it's not what she wanted at all. She wanted to be somewhere else, far away with him, where they could just spend time getting to know each other again. The fact that she'd always wanted him didn't mean it was the right thing. She couldn't convince her heart that it was anything other than the right thing, but sometimes it was hard to know what to do. And what she really didn't want to do was have him see her as Amy.

Astra settled into the vehicle, watching as the city disappeared behind them. It was hard to even keep track of the traffic, it moved so steadily, becoming part of the surroundings. "How is it people live like this?" she asked, as they finally exited London.

"I think they don't know any other way," Garret said. "Unless you deliberately tried to change or to make change happen, it's pretty hard without that."

"Meaning, it doesn't just happen accidentally. You have to actually focus on it?"

"Exactly," he said. "When you think about it, if they don't like this lifestyle, just identifying that is the start of getting out of it."

She nodded. "I know. That's one of the reasons why my job is shifting," she said. "I've been doing a lot of traveling around, but I'm trying to stay home more because I'm just tired of the damn airport."

"If a lot of the work you do is cyberstuff, can't you just stay home and do most of it?"

"I'm more of a liaison for one of the companies," she said. "I don't do any of the cyberhacking myself. I do the marketing, and I'm kind of a goodwill ambassador. I go to all these countries that we need cooperation from, in order to keep finding all these predators," she murmured.

"Are you dealing with pornography and child trafficking?"

She nodded but didn't look at him.

"That's tough," Garret said. "Really tough. That's the kind of thing most people don't want to deal with because it's so ugly."

"Which is why it's so important that somebody does deal with it," she said quietly. "A lot of children and young women have grown up in that abusive scenario, who don't know anything else."

"True enough," he said, "but, then again, you're making a difference, and that changes how you view your job too."

"It's what keeps me in it," she said, "but again, as far as making a change, I'm trying to scale back from a lot of the traveling."

"What brought that on?"

"Finding out my sister was pregnant, wondering if she would be a single mom," she admitted.

He winced at that. "God, I would hope not."

"We don't even know if Gregg's alive," she said.

"He's alive," Garret said. "We can't entertain any other

answer."

She nodded and sank deeper into her seat, pausing to look out the car window. "If we find her at the cabin, what will you say to her?" she asked.

"That I'll be there for her," he said simply.

"That would be you, wouldn't it?" she said, with a nod. "You can't do any less, can you?"

"No," he said. "Hell no. She needs support, love, and understanding, regardless of all the things that happened in the past. The child deserves nothing less than the best efforts from all of us."

"That child needs a family," she said, studying him.

"I know," he said. "I know."

Yet he didn't offer to be there, but then why would he? Astra didn't know if he was upset that the child was his brother's and not his. Either way, that had to bite. "The crazy webs we weave," she muttered to herself but didn't think he heard.

He looked at her and said, "Often it's a simple case of lies and deceit."

"But she didn't have to stay on that same track," she said.

"No, she didn't," he said. "I'm more than ready to get off it."

"You should have been off it a long time ago," she said.

He chuckled. "You're right, and I have been in many ways. Something about all this brought it all back."

"And it's a test," she said, "to see if you're really over her."

"I'm over her," he said, "but I'm still angry."

"But we're never angry for the reason we think we are," she murmured, repeating something she'd read somewhere.

"Sounds like New Age mumbo jumbo to me," he said. "I know why I'm angry, but that doesn't mean I've shared the reason."

"What the hell?" she said, looking at him in surprise. "What's this? You've actually done some deep soul-searching?"

"Of course," he said. "I won't repeat that mistake."

"Ah," she said. "So have you been single ever since?"

"No," he said. "Just very much unattached."

"There is a difference, isn't there?" she said, with a nod. "What about you?"

"No relationships that have mattered in quite a while," she said.

"How come?"

"Because," she said, with an easy laugh.

"Meaning, if I'm not sharing more, you're not sharing more?"

She shrugged. "Hardly the time or place."

This time, Kano popped into the conversation from the driver's seat. "Which usually means that, when it does happen, it's real."

"I don't know about that," she said. "Nothing about any of this feels for real."

"Just makes it all that much more important," Kano said. "Whatever you find at this level, that you survive at this stage in your life," he said, "it'll be there for a lot longer than you suspect."

"Doesn't mean I want to embrace it though," she said.

"I'm pretty sure it's already too late for that," he said, and he caught her gaze in the rearview mirror.

She realized, with a shock, that Kano already understood how she felt about Garret. She didn't know how Kano possibly could know, but he already instinctively knew. And, if he did, did Garret? Because that's not what she wanted. She shuffled back and stared out the window, her mind in a whirl.

Now what would she do? This was all just BS, if that was the case. She gave herself a stern talking to, straightened up as they slowed down, coming into the little seaside village. "If you head forward," she said, "and take that left up there"—pointing ahead—"it's about ten miles out."

"Interesting location."

"It's where my parents used to come all the time over the years, whenever they got the chance. Also, whenever they were having major difficulties, they'd come here, until they worked it out."

Garret looked at her, surprised, and said, "I kind of like that idea."

"It worked for them," she agreed.

"What happened to them?" Garret asked.

"My mom had breast cancer, pretty advanced, and she died. After that, my dad pretty well just drank himself to death," she said. "It wasn't cirrhosis of the liver or anything, but it might as well have been. He fell down the stairs stone cold drunk and cracked his head. He never regained consciousness and died four days later," she said.

"That must have been really tough on you guys. I'm sorry."

"It was," she said. "What's also tough is when parents just walk away because life is too hard. If it's too hard for them, imagine what it's like for the kids," she murmured.

"I don't think parents, when they're in that state, actually have the clarity to think things through. They're so bound by grief and every other emotion that's tearing them apart that all they can do is react."

Garret's words of insight surprised her. She looked at him for a long moment, then nodded and said, "You know what? That's as good of an explanation as anything."

"If you need one still," he said, with that gentle smile.

She hated that she still needed one, but sometimes she did need a reminder.

Kano pulled up outside a small cabin, twisting around to look at her. "Is this it?"

"Yes, we don't actually own the cabin anymore," she said. "It was just this little strip of land." She opened her door, hopped out, stood there, and stared.

"Does your family still own any property?" Kano asked.

"No, my dad drank away most of it," she said. "Neither of us are flush anymore."

"But you were raised with wealthy parents?" Kano faced her now.

"Not really. They were both working, so we were fine, but it's not like we could just jet set off for holidays everywhere or anything." She walked forward with a determined step.

"You might want to remember that other people could be living here then, right?" Garret offered.

There was a slight falter in her confidence, and she nodded. Very quickly both men stepped up to her side. The three of them walked around to the front of the cabin. They saw no sign that anybody was in residence.

"I wonder who even bought it," she murmured, looking around. "We had a lot of happy memories here."

"Sounds like your parents may have had some unhappy memories here too," Kano said.

"Maybe they started out that way," she said, "but they

worked it out, every time."

"I'll say it again," Garret replied. "I really like the idea of just going away together, until you can figure it out. That way, you don't involve everybody else, and you don't make decisions without having at least a worthy goal of trying to sort things through."

She walked up the steps to the front of the cabin and knocked, but she got no answer. She turned to look around at the lake and saw the other cabins dotting the property, connected by walkways, but it was tranquil, serene. Trees abounded, and a nice peaceful meadow was beyond them. She smiled. "It really does bring back memories."

"Maybe," Garret said. "But is your sister here?"

Startled and brought abruptly back to the reality of what they were doing here, she turned to the cabin and reached out a hand. The knob turned easily, and she pushed it open. She walked inside, both men at her side. "I don't know if anybody's here or not," she said. "It's pretty dark and empty." She walked into the kitchen and opened the fridge. "On the other hand," she called out, "I see ham, cheese, and milk in here."

"What are the dates on the milk?" Garret asked.

"Expires four days from now."

"So somebody is in residence," he said, and quietly he motioned at the loft above. Nodding, she immediately headed that way, Garret on her heels.

As soon as she got up to the top step, a cry came from inside.

"Who's there?"

"Amy, it's me, Astra," she said, as she stepped into her sister's room. Amy was inside a sleeping bag, on the floor of the main bedroom in the loft.

She looked up at Astra, pushing the hair off her forehead. "Why are you here?" she cried out.

"Maybe I should ask you that question," Astra said, as she walked over and crouched beside her sister. "Are you okay?"

"As much as I'll ever be," she said bitterly. But then her gaze landed on Garret, and she frowned. "And why are you here?" she asked bluntly. Right behind him was Kano. She shuffled backward, still in the sleeping bag, until she was up against the wall, looking as if she felt threatened.

Kano smiled at her gently and said, "Hello. I'm Kano, a friend of Garret's."

Her gaze once again shifted back to Garret. She frowned at him. "I didn't mean for you to come."

"Oh, come on. Of course you did," he murmured, as he leaned against the doorjamb across from Kano.

Astra turned to look at him and then back at Kano. "Maybe I should talk to my sister alone for a moment."

Garret immediately shook his head. "Not happening," he said. Astra gave him a hard frown, but he just frowned right back.

"Why did you run?" Garret asked Amy.

"I needed to," she said.

"Maybe so," he said, "but, by not giving anybody a chance to know where you were, we immediately suspected that you'd been taken, just like my brother. And that's why I'm here," he said. "To find out what you know about my brother's disappearance."

At that, Amy's bottom lip trembled. Still in the sleeping bag, she pulled her knees and the bag up against her chest, wrapped her arms tightly around them and said, "I don't know. I don't know anything."

"Are you sure about that?" her sister murmured.

Amy stared at her bitterly. "And just like that, you always have to argue with me, don't you?"

"Listen. You're the one who sent out the warning," Astra said. "I get over here just in time to find that you're missing and that nobody knows anything about you. You do know that the police have opened a missing person file on you, right?"

Amy just looked at her, and tears collected in the corners of her eyes. "Of course not. How would I possibly know that?" she said. "I came here to think."

"Well, now you'll get some help thinking," Garret said, as he motioned at the sleeping bag. "Why don't you get out and come downstairs, and we can sit and talk this over."

"I have nothing to talk about to you or to her," she snapped, glaring at him. "This has nothing to do with either of you."

"It has a lot to do with me, since my brother is missing," he said in a steely voice. "And you're the one who sounded the alarm. You can't just *unring* the bell and not produce my brother."

She started to sob then, and Astra gave a heavy sigh. "Come on. Let's get you downstairs. When did you eat last?"

Her sister shrugged, as Astra looked at the men in the doorway. "Look, guys. I'll bring her down in a minute. Let's give her a chance to get dressed."

She watched as the two men shifted back ever-so-slightly. She motioned with her hand. "Go, go, go."

Garret just glared at her.

"Stop the intimidation tactics," she snapped. "Let me get my sister dressed, and we'll come down."

"You've got five minutes," he bit off, as he turned and

headed down the stairs. "Don't let her run off again."

Astra closed the door, and her sister looked at her and said, "I don't know what I ever saw in him."

Astra, of course, knew exactly what it was because she herself still saw the same thing. "More to the point," Astra said, "He's not a man to make an enemy of, so hurry up and get dressed. Then we can go have a talk."

"I'm not going," Amy said. "You can't make me."

Astra stared at her sister, who was acting like a dramatic young child, and said, "Well, I guess I'll just bring them back up here then, and you can have this discussion while you're half dressed. But I was thinking you might feel better and have more confidence if you got dressed and came downstairs. Then we can all sit down, and you can tell us what the hell is going on."

"And I'm pretty sure that, once again, you didn't even listen to me," she said. "I told you. I don't know anything."

"Well, you knew enough to make contact with Garret's team, and, once you set that into motion, there is no going back."

"That's ridiculous," she said. "It's got nothing to do with him."

"Says you," Astra said, with a sigh. "Now, are you coming down, dressed, or shall I just call them back up?"

"Fine," her sister said, throwing back her sleeping bag and scrambling out. She wore just a T-shirt and panties. She quickly dressed and walked downstairs, ahead of her sister. "I don't need you guys here," she said. "You're just ruining everything."

"Well, I guess it depends what you mean by *ruining everything*," Astra answered, "because that's just crazy."

"No, it isn't," Amy said. "And again you don't listen."

"Says you," Astra groaned.

As the two sisters walked into the living room, still wrangling, Garret stood, looked at Amy, and said, "Now tell me the truth. Where's my brother?"

Instantly Amy burst into tears.

GARRET REMEMBERED THE tears. How was it that he couldn't forget the tears? He just glared at Amy and said, "Stop it."

But Amy wasn't listening, she was too far gone.

"You won't get answers out of her that way," Astra said, as she walked over and motioned for her sister to sit down. She walked into the kitchen, checked out the meager food supplies in the cupboard and the fridge, and said, "Looks like the only thing you can eat here is peanut butter and jam or ham and cheese."

"Well, she's not staying obviously," Garret said. "So it doesn't matter."

"I am too staying," Amy said, through her tears. She got up and, walking into the kitchen, she pulled out a loaf of bread, plopped down two slices, cut some cheese, and put it all together into a sandwich. She leaned against the counter, glaring at Garret, as she made her way through the sandwich.

Once again, she had him wondering what he'd ever seen in her.

"I don't know what happened to Gregg," she announced out of the blue.

"You said he disappeared," Garret said. "You knew that I would come. Obviously you had some reason for thinking that."

"Yes, he's not answering my calls or anything."

"Did he break up with you?"

"Of course not," she snapped. "That's not something he would do." He just raised an eyebrow at her. "Well, it isn't," she said.

"Does he know about the baby?" Garret asked Amy.

She gasped in horror. "What do you know about the baby?" she cried out. One hand went to her belly, as she spun to look at her sister.

Astra stared back. "Do you think people won't know?" she asked in surprise. "And, yes, I told him about the baby. For all I know, that's why Gregg disappeared."

"He wouldn't do that," she said. "He's a good man." Then she shot another sideways look at Garret, as if to suggest that he wasn't.

He rolled his eyes at that. "Yes, my brother's a good man. Especially when he's not screwing around with someone else's fiancée."

At that, her face turned beet red, and she said, "See? No point in having him here."

"Maybe not," Astra said, "but we're here because of Gregg, to find out what's going on with him. I came because you disappeared. He's here because his brother is gone."

"Well," Amy said, "Garret has all kinds of connections, so he can find Gregg on his own."

"Which is exactly why you contacted me," Garret said. "But I need more than *he's just not answering your calls.*"

She munched away furiously, filling her cheeks like a chipmunk as she chewed, and she said, "It was two days ago."

"What was two days ago?"

"I told him that I was pregnant. He was shocked, but I don't think he was terribly upset. I just think he didn't have time to sort his way through it all. He asked me what I wanted to do, and I said I didn't know. He got a phone call and told me that he had to leave for a meeting, but we would discuss it when he got back."

"But he didn't come back?"

"No," she said. "He didn't come back." And, once again, the tears welled up in her eyes. "I don't know what happened."

"What time of day was it?" Kano asked.

"Dinnertime," she said. "I held off telling Gregg until then."

"Why is that?" Kano said.

"Because I worried about it all day, wondering if I should even tell him or if I should just walk away."

"Why would you do that?" Garret said. "It's his child, after all." Then he stopped and said, "It is his child, isn't it?"

She shot him a baleful look. "Yes, it's his child, which makes you an uncle."

"What makes you think that he didn't just take off?" Kano asked, trying to insert a voice of reason.

"Because he's not that kind of a guy," she snapped. "He wouldn't leave me like this."

Kano looked at Garret, who shrugged, conceding the point. It wasn't what he would have expected of his brother, but that didn't mean that Gregg didn't need some time to clear his head and had walked away for a few days. "How does he typically contact you?"

"On my phone, or he could come home of course. We've been living together for the last year." She shot Garret a hard look. "Like you don't already know that."

"I don't know anything about you guys," he said. "I haven't had any contact with my brother since we broke up."

Her gaze widened. "Wow, what a surprise. And you being all about family."

"Until I found out you had changed the family roles behind my back," he said. "Instead of dealing with it head-on and telling me—preferably before you started sleeping with my brother."

She glared at him. "You can insult me all you want," she said, "but, Garret, you don't understand."

"Probably not," he said, tired of the whole mess. "The bottom line is that he's my brother, and he's missing. I'll do my best to find him, if I can."

A little bit of hope clung to her gaze, and she asked, "Do you know how?"

"Well, if you can't give me any more than what you've given me so far," he said, "it'll be damn hard."

She just frowned at him again.

He groaned. "You've got to tell me a little more about that phone call. Was a name mentioned? Did it seem like it was somebody he knew? Did it sound like a work call or what?"

She frowned. "I'm not sure," she said. "I mean that for real because he never talked about work."

"Where were you living?"

"Belgium," she said. "I wanted to move back to England, but he didn't want to."

"Of course not," he said. "Why did you want to come to England?"

Just as she was about to launch into this big tirade, he stopped her and said, "Never mind. The fact is, you were still in Belgium when it happened. So where in Belgium were you living?"

She gave him the address, and he said, "How long did

you live there?"

"One year," she said.

"So why did you run to England?"

"Because I wanted the baby born here," she said.

Astra just stared at her. "What? You're hardly even showing yet. You had plenty of time. The minute your boyfriend doesn't answer your phone calls, you come running to England. Why?"

"Because he told me to," she said resentfully.

"When?" Garret asked, and now he was all business. "You said you'd had no contact."

"Because of his work, he told me that, if anything ever happened to him, that I should leave, take nothing, and just go to London."

"Well, that's generally good advice," he said, "but it's not helpful at all in terms of finding him."

"Well, he knew I wouldn't find him anyway. I was supposed to go, to save myself." She just stared at him, offended by his incredulous stare. "Like you wouldn't have done the same."

"No," he said. "I wouldn't have, but I can understand my brother telling you to." He stared at Kano, looking for a clear perspective. "Suggestions?"

"Get back to civilization, where we can access our laptops, and figure out what we need to do."

"We can do some of that here too," Astra said. "An internet café is not very far from here. Otherwise no internet is around this area, unless you can get it on your phone."

"Which we can," Garret said, "but Kano is probably looking to do a much bigger search. Those databases are very bandwidth heavy, and we could be pinpointed, if somebody were looking for us."

"Why the hell would anybody even know you're here?" Amy said. "That's ridiculous!"

"Because you called," he said. "That immediately sends people alerts, especially if they're after us."

She snorted. "God, why is everything always about you?" she said. "This has nothing to do with you."

"Well, I hope that's true, but you're also the one who left a message saying you thought Gregg had something to do with my accident. The plane crash. Remember?"

She flushed bright red at that. "No," she said. "I didn't mean that."

"*Seriously?*" He stared at her, his heart sinking. "Then why did you say it?"

"He told me that you'd had a bad accident, but that nobody was talking and wouldn't tell him anything. I figured, if you wouldn't come because he was missing, you might come if it meant you could get your revenge on him."

"Jesus Christ, Amy," he said, rubbing his face with both hands. "Look. I don't waste energy on revenge," he said, his gaze narrowing. "You two are together now, and I'm just glad to be out of the whole triangle mess." Immediately her back stiffened, as she just glared at him. "The bottom line is," he said, "that my brother is missing, and that's why I'm here."

"Are you telling me it's not because you thought you could actually get answers about the accident?"

"Answers would have been nice," he said. "And it certainly would justify Kano being here too. But, as usual, we're dealing with your lies and deceit. I told him that we couldn't trust anything that came out of your mouth."

"But you came anyway?"

"*My brother is missing.* How many times do I have to say

that?" he said, trying to exercise patience. "No matter the circumstances with you, I need to find him. Dealing with a lying, cheating person like you makes it more complicated because I can't believe anything you say, but I still have to get him back."

"Why do you keep insulting me like that?" she said.

"I'm not insulting you at all," he snapped. "It's the truth, Amy. If you don't like it, you shouldn't act that way."

"For the love of God, you two," Astra said, "can we get back on track here, instead of hashing out all your old crap?"

"Gladly," Garret said. "If your sister has nothing to offer, I'm out of here."

"Wait," Astra said, as she raced behind him. When he looked down at her, she frowned. "My sister is still in trouble."

"I don't know why," he said, tilting his head.

"That's because you're still in a haze of anger," she murmured. "And I get that. I really do. But remember the people at the hotel? No matter what you're feeling about Amy right now, she's carrying Gregg's baby—maybe the last bit of him you'll ever have."

He froze, closed his eyes, and, leaning against the porch wall, said, "Shit."

CHAPTER 6

W HAT ASTRA HAD heard actually made her feel better. Because all this back-and-forth was just a sign of having an outlet for that anger, that initial rage Garret needed to vent. But no love was in his tone, nor any love in his gaze, as he stared at Amy. He appeared to be really over his relationship with her sister. That was good news.

What wasn't good news was that he was right. Her sister, true to form, had lied and cheated to get Garret over here. But why? Because his brother was missing, and she thought that he wouldn't care enough, which in itself proved that she didn't really understand Garret all that much. And, once again, he held it against her for having deceived him. He was desperate to find out who was after his team. Whether that involved his brother or not didn't make it a priority over everything else going on, including the fact that Garret's own life was still in danger.

Astra reached up, patted Garret's cheek, and said, "Honestly I wouldn't have brought it up, but for the fact that she's my sister."

He opened his gaze, nodded slowly, and said, "And I can't let go of the idea that it's all still related to Gregg's disappearance."

"And, Garret," she said, dropping her voice even lower. "I'm sorry that she lied. I know you're desperate to find out what's going on with the assault on your team, but we don't know for sure if Gregg's disappearance is even related. Although I would think that anything to do with Kingdom Securities is suspicious at this point."

He stared at her, his gaze lowered, but she could see the cogs and the wheels turning in his brain. "You're right," he said thoughtfully. "We've got a search running on that company, but I think we need to deepen it."

"I've got one running too," she said, "but I'm not getting anything."

He looked at her in surprise.

She shrugged. "Think about what I do," she said. "I can pretty well get most things analyzed, but it's not exactly the same field, and I can't necessarily claim to have budget money for something like this, since it's not about cases in the cybersex world."

He smiled, nodded, and said, "Well, my budget isn't limited to just those kinds of assholes. Ours covers all kinds of assholes."

"Good for you," she said. "Sometimes I wish I could do more."

"You're doing what you can, and, if everybody just did that," he said, "we could turn the tide."

"Instead, everybody does what they can do on the opposite side of life," she said, "but I can't leave my sister in this scenario."

"I know," he said. "Besides, she's carrying my niece or nephew."

"Exactly," Astra said and was grateful that he seemed to have turned a mental corner and was getting past his old anger. Because this wasn't the time. Astra understood his anger, but this wasn't the time to start airing more grievances. She knew it would happen again, when they found his brother, assuming Gregg was alive. But Garret still had so much hurt inside that he would have to deal with it and with Gregg at some point. But, if she could help mitigate some of that in the meantime, it would make life easier on them all. She turned back to look at Kano, who was busy on his phone. "Can you get what you need here?"

"To a certain extent, but we need information. We've got people on it, but they're not exactly getting what we need right now fast enough."

"Can you find it faster?" she asked.

He looked at her, surprised. "It's hard to say," he said, "but I don't have what I need here. The internet's just funky enough, and my phone isn't the best thing for accessing some of these databases." He walked back into the living room, where Amy was curled up in the chair. "We need addresses for where he's been living, where he works, his license plates, anything you can tell us about his friends and other cohorts."

Her sister supplied as much of the information as she could, and she had a much more mollified attitude now, enough so that Astra wondered if Kano had said something to her.

"Now that you have whatever you deem as important," Amy said, "you can leave."

"I can," Garret said, quite happily, "but I'll make this one-time offer. You can come with us and stay safe, or you can stay here and do you."

"That's easy. I'll stay here and do me," she said instantly in a sarcastic tone.

"That's fine," he said. "I will also tell you this only once. Somebody was watching the hotel room you disappeared from."

She stared at him and asked, "What do you mean?"

"Somebody," Astra said, immediately stepping in, "was watching your hotel room. When we went in, they came in too, and they tried to attack us."

Amy looked from one to the other in confusion. "Why do they care?"

"Well, that's what we were hoping you could tell us," Garret said. "Somebody is either looking for my brother and thinks you have information, or, because they already have my brother, they're looking for you for leverage."

"Leverage?" her voice squeaked.

"Yes," he said. "Leverage. To make my brother talk."

"And why would he do that?"

"Well, that's a good question," he said, "but, if they have you, they can hurt you and can get Gregg to reveal what they want before they hurt you too badly."

She just stared at him, her hands going to her belly, her skin suddenly pale.

"You didn't have to say it quite that way," Astra said to him quietly.

"No easy way to tell her," he said. "She's in trouble, whether she wants to admit it or not."

"But I don't know anything," Amy said.

"Well, they won't care because my brother does know a lot," he said. "If anybody knows that you lived with him, which I assume they do, then they'll know that you might have information they could possibly use."

"So what am I supposed to do?" she said.

"Hope that we weren't followed," Kano said quietly. "Hope that not too many people know about this place."

She stared at him blankly. "I don't know who might

know, but I've never tried to hide anything."

"Which is why it's interesting that my brother was living with you," he said, "because he should have known better. He should have known that he was putting you in danger." He tilted his head to the side. "Was he there all the time?"

Slowly she shook her head. "No, not all the time, only when he could get away, which wasn't often," she admitted slowly.

"Where did he stay the rest of the time?" Kano asked immediately.

She glared at him.

"This isn't about your relationship," Astra said, getting frustrated with her sister. "This is about all of it, and you have to do what you can to keep the baby safe."

"Like you care about the baby," she snapped.

Astra groaned. "Let's not bring up any more about family crap, okay? Let's just deal with the facts at hand."

"Wouldn't that be nice?" Garret said. "The facts are that somebody was hunting you at the hotel, and others could be coming here to look for you."

"Well, what happened to the ones at the hotel?" Amy asked.

"MI6 has them now," Astra answered.

"But Gregg says MI6 is bad," Amy said. "You just gave the enemy to the enemy?"

"Interesting that he would say that," Garret said, "because we tend to have a dim view of MI6, but that's only because they're another band of authority. None of us like having to play all these games, but I wouldn't have said they were bad."

"That just goes to prove that your brother is smarter than you," she said, with spirit, as if loving the fact that she could say something that might get to him.

"So here's your chance. I'm heading out the front door right now," Garret said, turning, walking outside, with Kano right behind him. "Either come along or stay here."

Astra ran behind him. "Surely you won't just leave her like that?"

"What do you want me to do?" he said, turning to look at her with surprise. "I'm not going to kidnap her. She's already called the cops on me once, and I'm not giving her the ammunition to do that again."

She winced. "She's still carrying your niece or nephew, and she still might know something valuable about your brother. Think about the information she just gave you now."

"You mean, the fact that she lied again, and that Gregg wasn't actually living with her?"

Astra winced. "I know," she said, "but we did get information we needed."

"What do you want me to do?" he said.

"I want you to put aside your past grievances. If this were me, what would you do?"

He looked at her in surprise, then shrugged and said, "I wouldn't give you a choice. I'd pick you up, toss you in the car, and take you along."

"And why is that?"

He grinned, leaned over, and whispered, "Because I care about what happens to you."

With that, he headed to the car, leaving her in shock.

THE LOOK ON Astra's face was priceless and worth every word. The thing is, Garret also meant it. He did care. He wasn't sure exactly how much because it seemed like nothing was normal anymore, and his system was flooded with anger and hurt—that sense of betrayal, that sense of not being able to trust. But then just the thought of all those negative thoughts applied to Astra didn't work at all. He knew that his thinking was skewed because of his experience with her sister, but Astra was a completely different kettle of fish.

He'd already run several checks on her since he'd arrived. Everything had come back positive. Everybody who worked with her loved her. She had a little bit of a history with a past relationship that was concerning, but that nagged at him more because Garret wanted to beat the crap out of the guy.

She had called for assistance at one point in time, and, when the police arrived, they took the boyfriend away for making death threats against her. He disappeared from view shortly afterward and hadn't popped up anywhere, so Garret wasn't exactly sure of the where, what, and how, but that was one year ago. So this guy was really off the radar or not around at all.

Garret wasn't certain how badly affected she had been, and that was always a concern for him. But the thought of coming back here and getting tied up in another relationship that was as traumatic as the one with her sister was something Garret didn't want to do.

Immediately that same voice of reason reminded him that it wouldn't be the same because Astra was a completely different person. She had a career of her own and a life of her own. She had been through relationships and understood the trauma of the breakups.

It was a completely different scenario, and he had to remember to give her the chance to get over whatever it was that needed to be dealt with. Because some things in life were worth the wait. And that included his own ability to open himself back up to being hurt again, if that's what he chose to do. That's not what he wanted to think about, but it was definitely there in front of them, and the longer he looked at Astra, and the more he was around her, the bigger the issue became. As he stood outside, staring at the sky, Kano joined him.

"What are you thinking about, looking like that?" Kano asked.

"I like Astra," he said, "and I can sure as hell see why I don't want anything to do with Amy anymore, although, apparently at the time, I couldn't see it for some reason."

"Because you had it all worked out," Kano said. "Like you always used to do. You'd have a plan ten steps ahead of where we were, before anybody else even got close to it. You probably figured it was time to get married, and that was just the way it would go."

"Makes me sound like a real jerk," Garret said. "I guess maybe I rushed her. Clearly I didn't realize what I was getting into or what I was pushing her into."

"Relationships can be like that," Kano said. "Doesn't mean the next one will be though."

"No," he said. "That's true." Just then, Astra and her sister came out, but instead of even looking at Amy, his gaze was locked on to Astra. "I like her," Garret muttered to Kano.

"She's a much better choice for you."

"No choice involved," he said. "I know it, and that's how I can tell how serious I am." At that, he looked at Kano, shook his head, and said, "Wait. That's not what I meant."

"I know that too," he said, as he smiled and shook his

head. "I'm driving."

"I want to drive," Garret said, not willing to give over the driver's side door.

"Nope," Kano said. "You need to sort yourself out a little more. Besides, I think we need to head to Charles's."

"With the women?"

"Yeah, we need a place to hide, and that's as good as we can get."

"Right," he said. "I guess I should call him then."

"Exactly."

After Garret helped the two women into the car, he stepped away a few steps and called Charles.

"There you are," Charles said. "Are you coming this way?"

"We're about ninety minutes out," he said. "Maybe a little bit longer. I'm not alone."

"Good enough. Do you know how to get in?"

He smiled. "I do, and I'll send you a text when we're close." He hung up and walked over to see that Kano was already in the driver's seat. Garret got into the vehicle, and they started back into London. He looked at Astra. "Did you grab everything she had there?"

Amy glared at him, speaking of her like she wasn't even here.

Astra held up the bag with the few groceries and the sleeping bag. "Yes, we've got it all."

"Good," he said.

"Where are we going now?" Astra asked.

"To a friend of ours," he said. "Somebody who's got a safe place for us to spend a few days."

"I hate to intrude," Astra murmured.

"Sure," he said.

"I'm assuming this is kind of the work he does too, so he's used to people bunking down whenever they need to?" Astra asked.

"If that's what we need to do," he said. "He works with several groups that I know over in the US, plus Bullard's camp in Africa."

"Bullard?" Amy said. "That was something he said."

Garret spun around and looked at her. "Who said that, and what was said?"

Amy stared at him in confusion. "I'm not exactly sure, but there was some mention of Bullard as part of the conversation on the phone call before Gregg left."

"Huh," he said. "You don't remember any more of it?"

She shook her head. "No, I'm sorry. I don't even remember what it was. I just caught that last little bit of a name."

"Was Gregg laughing, joking, angry?"

"No, it was more like an 'Okay, so Bullard's in it,' or whatever."

"Is that what he said?"

"No," she said. "He didn't say that, but it was something like that, and that was the tone of the conversation."

"Right, so nothing to give you any kind of feeling about it?"

She shrugged and said, "No, I didn't spend any time on it. I knew his work was dangerous, and it was his stuff, so I didn't get involved."

Her tone was suddenly morose, realizing that she should have, over the last three years, gotten a little more involved. But Garret could hardly blame her. As it was, he knew perfectly well that his brother was really good at keeping people out of his life. That's how they worked and lived. It was part of the job. He glanced back at Astra and murmured, "We need to know everything."

She nodded and settled back with her sister.

He turned and looked out the front windshield, one ear listening to the conversation in the back. But they'd already turned to discussions about the baby.

"Did you pick out a name?"

"No," Amy said. "That's something I was hoping to do with Gregg."

Her sister's voice broke, and he heard the authenticity of emotion threading through Amy's tone. If nothing else, she may actually love Gregg. And, for that, he was grateful. Because it would really be terrible to think she was screwing Gregg over too. Garret had already asked Amy if the baby was actually Gregg's, and, despite her claim it was, Garret still doubted her word. It was hard for him to not consider it, considering what she'd done to him. But this wasn't the time or place. He found it interesting that Astra had as much patience with her sister as she did.

CHAPTER 7

ASTRA WASN'T PART of the same shadowy underworld as these guys. At least not in the real world. Thankfully she was at least one step removed from the dirty details of her job. All her work involved cyberstuff, but, even then, she didn't do the hacking. She was part of the front company that worked on investors and alliances with other countries. They certainly needed cooperation between countries in order to catch some of these assholes. Now here she was, seeing firsthand what this cyberworld looked like in the real physical world as they went around the block twice.

She leaned forward and asked, "Why are—?"

Garret held up a hand, and then, on the third pass, a garage door opened. The garage door was there so suddenly, and they made such a sharp turn, that it caused her and her sister to slide against each other. She frowned as they abruptly disappeared downward, off the main street, into an underground parking lot.

She looked at him. "What? Is this spy stuff?"

"Absolutely it's spy stuff," he said, turning to shoot her a smile. The area was dark, with fluorescent lights flicking on overhead as they pulled into one of what looked like easily a dozen parking spots.

As soon as they were parked, her sister hopped out and looked around. "Is Gregg here?"

"Why would Gregg be here?" Astra asked in surprise.

Her sister's shoulders slumped. "I don't know. I just figured he was into this superspy stuff, and maybe he was here too."

"As far as I know," Garret said. "Gregg is not here." He thought about it and wondered just what Charles might know. Garret led the way to an elevator. He punched the elevator button. In front of them on the nearby wall was a security keypad, and its cover opened up. Astra watched in surprise as Garret punched in a code that had the double doors to the elevator opening, which led into the elevator itself. With all four of them inside, he shut the doors and took them up.

The elevator buttons noted three floors, and Astra didn't get that, since one floor should have been street level, so where were they going? As soon as the doors opened, they walked out into what looked like a living room.

He smiled and said, "Now we take the stairs." They went down a set of stairs, and, at a door that looked like it might go to a bedroom, he opened it up and knocked on what looked to be a wall on the other side. Immediately a hidden door opened, and everybody was ushered through.

As she watched, Garret carefully pulled the first door closed, locked it, and then they closed the second door. She was in a completely different townhome, from the looks of it. She stared around in surprise, her gaze landing on their host. Charles was a silver-haired man and still had a heavy dash of verve in his gaze, for a sixty-something male. She reached out a hand to shake his and said calmly, "Hi, I'm Astra, and this is my sister, Amy."

"And I am Charles, at your service," he said, with a courtly bow. She was charmed.

He led the way into a living room, and he said, "Please be seated. We'll have tea." Then Charles left the room.

Astra sat down, always amused at the British answer to every situation. But, as she checked the time, she found it was actually tea time for them.

Her sister sat down uncomfortably on the seat beside her. She looked around at the heavy brocade furnishings from an era gone by. "What is this place?" Amy asked suspiciously.

Astra patted her gently on the knee. "This is Charles's home," she said quietly, "so please treat it and him with respect."

Her sister glared at her and slumped backward on the couch.

Garret looked at Astra and nodded in approval. "It is, indeed, Charles's home. His granddaughter lives here sometimes, when she comes to visit, but, other than that, he's here alone."

"Interesting," Astra said. "Is he likely to have any information for us?"

At that, Charles's voice chimed in, as he came down the hallway. "Depends on what information you're looking for," he said. "I do get a lot of information, and some might surprise you."

"My brother," Garret said, "he's missing."

"I heard that," he said. "I'm sorry."

"But you haven't heard anything about it?"

"No, I haven't, but we do have feelers out." Charles walked over to the ladies and set a tray down on the coffee table in front of them. "The tea will help fortify you."

Amy looked at him in disgust. "Fortify? Nobody uses that language."

Charles laughed gently. "That's true. I'm a relic of times gone by, though that doesn't mean it's any less valid."

Astra gave her sister a look that clearly stated Astra was ashamed of Amy's words, and that was a damn good thing because they'd been taught better than to insult their host. Astra smiled and admitted, "Thank you. A cup of tea sounds perfect."

"A cup of tea is perfect, any time, my dear," he said, with the gentlest of smiles. "Your rooms are ready, should you need a nap or just even to lie down or freshen up for a bit."

"That would be lovely," Astra said.

Amy looked around and said, "I'm not even sure where we are."

"South of London," he said smoothly. "Not to worry, you're safe and we have your luggage with us."

She glanced at him and asked, "What street?"

"Do you need to know?"

Astra smiled and said, "No, she does not need to know." She wasn't sure why her sister was being so difficult, but, given her condition and what she'd been through, maybe it made sense. "I'll take you upstairs," she said to her sister.

"You don't even know where the upstairs is," Amy snapped.

She looked at Charles and said, "I'm sorry. My sister is pregnant." Then she let her voice drop away.

"Sure, let my pregnancy be the excuse for my manners," Amy said, with an eye roll.

"It would be nice if *something* was," Garret said, his tone much less amiable than before.

Amy glared at him and sank back again onto the couch. But a yawn caught her sideways. Surprised, she said, "I guess

I am more tired than I thought."

"Pregnancies will do that to you," Charles said.

This time, at least, she didn't dare insult him with another smart remark. He motioned at the tray on the sideboard and said, "I did bring some treats, in case anybody would like a pastry."

Immediately Astra sat up and asked, "Are those honest-to-goodness cream scones?"

He gave her a beaming smile. "They are, indeed."

Kano hopped up and said, "You have no idea how good his cream scones are. This man's a genius when it comes to baking."

"Do you have a recipe that's really good?" Astra asked. "I never seem to make them taste quite right."

Charles immediately hopped up, walked over, and pushed the tea cart closer. Then placed a large tray with cream scones and other treats on the coffee table in front of the ladies, with a plate of saucers and knives. "Help yourself, my dear. You tell me if it's a recipe you would like, and I'd be happy to share."

Eagerly, Astra reached for one, broke it in half, and just took a sniff, rolling her eyes in joy. "Now this looks wonderful." She put a little bit of butter on the side, took a tiny bite, and moaned in joy. "Delicious," she announced.

"Aw, for crying out loud," Amy said. But she leaned forward, picked up a scone, and, after she cut it and buttered both sides liberally, she sat back. Once she demolished it in a few bites, she reached for a second and finally a third. She stared down at her empty plate.

The three others looked at him, and Charles said, "They must have been delicious."

"I've never eaten so many in my life."

He just gave her a paternal smile and said, "Babies will do that."

She just continued to stare in surprise.

But Astra was happy that Amy had eaten at least. It didn't look like she'd touched much of the food she had brought to the cabin, certainly not enough to sustain anybody, not to mention a pregnant somebody. Still, her sister being amiable was a whole lot easier to deal with than her sister being rude. A few moments later Astra asked if it would be okay if they went up to their bedrooms.

"Of course," Charles said. "Follow me."

When they all trooped up behind him, even the men, Astra looked at Garret and said, "You don't need to come."

He gave her a smile and followed behind her. She still wasn't sure what to think of him and his behavior, but it was pretty hard to do anything, given the way they were acting now. Upstairs, the women were shown to two bedrooms on the right, with the men given two bedrooms on the left. Surprised, but happy to see the divine quality of the rooms, Astra smiled and said to her sister, "Why don't you go lie down for a bit? It will make you feel better."

Amy shrugged and said, "Why not? I ate so much that I'm tired." Stepping inside, she shut the door in their faces.

Astra looked back at Garret, shrugged, and said, "Do you want me to disappear? I can go spend some time in my room."

"No," he said. "You're fine."

She frowned. "Are you sure? Do you guys need some private time?"

"It's fine," he said. "Come on down, and we'll talk."

Back downstairs again, with her sister settled in her room, Astra motioned at the tray and said, "Charles, would you mind terribly if I had another one?"

He said, pleased, "Absolutely not, please have more. I'm delighted that you're enjoying them."

"Thank you," she said, with a smile, then watched as the other two men helped themselves to more and soon had demolished the rest of the plateful as well.

"This is great," she said to Charles. "I would love the recipe."

"Not a problem," he said. "I'll get it for you in a few minutes." He sat back, looked at the two men, and asked, "So any news?"

"No, and it's very, very frustrating."

"Of course it is," he said. "Nothing quite like family to both infuriate and impress."

At that, Garret smiled and said, "You're right. It's just been a while, and it seems like one thing after another in my world."

"This too will pass," he said, "although I suppose it's frustrating."

"Of course it is, but we'll get information. It's only a matter of time." Just then Garret's phone rang with an incoming text.

"Anything?" Kano asked.

He checked the message, then smiled and said, "Apparently there is facial recognition data of my brother in Belgium, after the point in time that he was kidnapped."

"*If* he was kidnapped," Charles said.

"Exactly," Garret replied. "There is some concern regarding his disappearance. That evening, as he supposedly walked away to attend a meeting, he was picked up by facial recognition after leaving Amy's place. He got into his vehicle and went down to a pub," he said, reading the information slowly. He then read off the address where the pub was located.

Immediately Kano brought it up, and Charles walked over to a big wall above the fireplace, pushed some buttons, and a huge screen opened up.

Astra laughed in delight. "I love it."

Garret grabbed the remote and brought up the address on the much bigger screen. They all gathered around to see where it was. He picked up his phone, dialed the texting number, and said, "Hey, Fallon. Where's his car now?"

"Abandoned, on the side street. Somebody moved it from the original position, so it wasn't initially picked up. Then it was towed by the police, as they tried to locate him."

"And, of course, he went nowhere, right?" Garret asked.

"Exactly, he doesn't appear to come out of the pub at any point in time."

"So, in theory, he's still there?" she asked.

"No," Garret said. "There'll be another entrance or exit to the place."

"Great," she muttered. "How do we find him now?"

"Has his face popped up anywhere yet?" Garret asked Fallon.

"No," Fallon replied. "No credit cards, bank accounts, nothing is being used."

"What about the joint account he has with his girl-friend?"

"No," Fallon said. "Nothing."

"She'd been warned by Gregg to avoid using the ac-counts," Garret muttered.

"And how well do you trust this person?" Fallon asked, from the other end of the call.

Garret glanced at Astra and said, "Most of the time, not

much. However, in this instance, there's no reason for her to lie."

There was a pregnant pause on the other end, as Fallon digested that. "Okay," he said in a neutral tone. "I'll take your word on that."

Kano piped up and said, "I actually agree with Garret in this instance, if that matters."

At that, with a little more relief in his voice, Fallon said, "Okay, so she's either running on cash or has her own bank account."

Astra popped up then, adding, "I'm sure she has her own bank account as well, but she's lying down right now, so I can't ask her."

"Good enough," he said. "It would be nice to find out for sure though, so we can see if that's something else we should be tracking."

"Fine," she said, glancing toward the stairway, but, of course, there was no sound from above.

"What we could really use is more information on where Gregg could be," Garret said.

"There may be a break on that side," Fallon said. "Do you remember Deedee, who was managing Kingdom Securities? She still is, as far as I know. She's the one who had a slight issue with Bullard?"

"Yes, what about her?"

"There is a chance that she's willing to talk."

"About what?"

"Well, the message I got was one she sent through the underground, saying she had nothing to do with it."

"Well, that sounds suspicious," Astra said.

Beside her, Charles immediately nodded.

Fallon continued on Speakerphone, "The issue, I think,

is the fact that people are suspicious, and, because of her falling out with Bullard, they're looking to her. So she's saying she didn't have anything to do with it and is willing to help with the investigation."

"Well, let's put some pressure on that," Garret said.

"I'd like to," Fallon said. "You're busy trying to find your brother, and, as far as we know, that could be related."

"Well, considering my brother may have had some association with her as well, maybe that's somebody we should be pushing," he said.

"Agreed, but, so far, I haven't gotten an answer from her," Fallon said.

"Does anybody over here have any connection with her?" Garret asked.

"She doesn't trust anybody," Fallon said.

"She trusts me," Kano said.

"Why the hell would she do that?" Garret asked, looking at him in surprise.

He shrugged. "We have some history—no, not sexually—but she was involved in the family for a time."

"Interesting," he said. "You've never mentioned it."

"I wouldn't be mentioning it now, if there was any way not to," he said. "I'd like to think she doesn't have anything to do with the attacks on our team, but I can't prove it."

"Send a message then, and see if she'll talk to us … or you."

"I've already done that," Kano said. "At the time, she didn't respond because it was me going to her about your missing brother."

"Why would she not respond?" Astra asked. "I don't get it."

"She'll want something, and just because we have a history doesn't mean I like her," he said. "She's not a very likable person."

At that, Astra frowned. "It sounds like it, but even assholes will usually talk business, won't they? So let's talk business."

"Maybe, but, if we could find the answers without her, that would be better. Then we can utilize whatever leverage we come up with in order to get answers on what's going on with Bullard."

"Right. That's your game anyway."

"It's one part of the game," Kano said. "Remember. That's only part of why we came here."

She nodded but felt a chill come over her shoulders at the reminder. "It all seems pretty messed up right now."

"No, it is totally messed up right now," Garret said, as he rang off from Fallon's call and turned to look at Charles, an odd look on his face. "Charles, what's up?"

"That Belgium pub you mentioned earlier, that your brother went into?" he said. "We have one here by the same name." He was busy working on the computer and viewing the monitor above the fireplace. "I wonder if it's related?"

"Yeah, but there are a million pubs with the same names, all around the world," Astra said.

"Yes, and it happens to be a great way to keep track of business, so people don't have any problems moving stuff from one location to the other."

"Meaning, they're connected somehow, like a franchise or something?"

"That's certainly a possibility. I hadn't considered the idea that they might have made the association legal."

"There are advantages to having a business be legal like that," she murmured.

"There can be disadvantages too," Garret said, as he studied the name of the place. "Maybe we should go pay this one a visit?"

"I think that's a grand idea," Charles said. "I'm not so sure this is all that innocent, if you look at it closely. Just see where it's situated."

They all studied the screen for a long moment.

"It's on the outskirts of town," Garret noted, "close to a main highway, close to the waterways for moving stuff in and out, and close to shipping lanes. But then, the location of a pub is important, like a gas station."

"Yes," Kano said. "Location, location, location."

"But it's also good for easily moving goods and materials," Charles noted.

At that, Kano turned to look at him, asking, "What kinds of goods and materials?"

Charles shook his head. "I've been working with MI6 on sex trafficking in England," he said. "We have a real problem that we're trying to lock down. We were looking for this type of location, and this looks ideal to me."

"If there's ever such a thing that's ideal," Astra murmured.

"Oh, absolutely there is, but, in this case," he said, "I wasn't thinking of Garret's brother, as much as this other problem."

"In case you don't know," Garret said. "Astra works in cybersecurity, hunting cyber-predators."

Charles looked at her in surprise. "I'm really glad to hear that. It's such a sad world out there."

"I know," she said. "We're working on it."

"Of course you are," he said warmly. "It'll take a whole lot more than just a couple of us to do this."

"It will," she said, feeling a kinship she hadn't expected. She studied the pub on the screen and said, "So I suggest we go get a beer then."

"I do too," Charles said. "So, my dear, would you like to come have a beer with me?"

Not sure what he was up to, she nodded in agreement. "I'd be honored, but what about these two?"

"Oh, we'll be there," Garret said. "Just not out front."

"Are you going hunting?" Astra asked.

"Absolutely," he said, giving her a hard smile. "We'll do the best kind of hunting there is."

"I'm not sure I like the sound of that," she said slowly.

"You'll be safe," he said. "I promise."

"You can't promise something like that," she said. "We have no connection linking Gregg to this particular pub, other than the name."

"Ah, maybe not," Kano said, looking up from his phone. "What we do have is the pub owner's name, who is the father of one of the men who works for Kingdom."

"Here we go again," Garret said. "Everything keeps coming back to Kingdom."

"It seems that way, doesn't it? So let's go pay that pub a visit."

DRESSED IN BLACK and already in the alleyway outside of the pub, Garret and Kano had pulled out the blueprints, searching for the secret entrance, knowing it had to be somewhere close by. They weren't exactly sure where, but there had to be some entrance they hadn't seen. Charles and Astra had gone in for a beer, and after discussing the plan with Amy—and getting her personal banking information, with more than a little resistance—had left her at Charles' home to rest.

The place was locked, so she couldn't leave; that was another safeguard Charles had in place. Her sister had agreed with that, and Garret had to admit, he was grateful that Amy hadn't caused a stink over it, especially since she had already pulled a fast one and taken off on them earlier. They didn't want her doing it again. Garret had explained to Astra that they couldn't afford to waste time looking for Amy, when everyone should be looking for his brother. She hadn't argued and had just agreed.

So now Garret and Kano were positioned in the back alley, looking for an entrance. Hearing a sharp whistle, he turned to see Kano, pointing down at a grate. It lifted easily, no noise at all. It was also made of a lighter-weight material than it should have been, and, except for an occasional vehicle parked directly on top of it, it probably didn't get much weight on it on a regular basis.

They quickly lifted the fake grate and set it aside, and, with the flashlight shining down, they used the ladder to get to the bottom. Just before he went farther down, Kano pulled the grate into place above his head. Someone here must know about this. It was just too unbelievable, but it was also good news for them. Down at the bottom they saw a series of tunnels.

"This is more like it," Garret said. "We were looking for something just like this."

They followed the path to the right, toward the pub. The pathway was angled, with a ditch runoff in the center, but it wasn't a culvert for sewage by any means.

"I wonder how long this has been down here?" Garret asked.

"Probably from way back when, maybe two, three hundred years ago," Kano said. "The building is at least that old. And it's not all that uncommon to have secondary entrances and exits to get into some of these places."

"No, it's not that uncommon," he said.

"Think how much easier life would be if we didn't have to put these kinds of things into a lot of the buildings we inhabit."

"Well, the thing is, most people don't have to do that," Garret said.

They headed in the direction of the pub and eventually found a small round door that looked odd to them. It was locked, so they quickly picked the lock and slipped inside. They heard voices above and glanced at each other and smiled when they realized they were underneath the pub.

"Noisy place to be keeping a prisoner though," Garret whispered.

"No way to know if the prisoner's actually here or not," Kano said. "Why would they keep him here? Seems too obvious."

He nodded at that. "Still, it's odd."

"As always," Kano said, "heads-up."

Right, they could never trust anything in this world—always too many cases of shit going wrong—but that was the nature of the business. As they moved in through the basement, they did a quick search, but they found no sign of Garret's brother ... or anyone else. Not that Garret had expected it to be that easy, but he couldn't help but hope to get lucky for once. They searched this whole level and found nothing. They made their way to the stairs, only to find that still another alcove was halfway above.

They quickly slipped into that to check it out. As they

did, they heard voices directly above them. "I don't give a shit what you think you want for keeping this guy. He's our prisoner, and we'll hang on to him and look after him until we need him," he said.

"The guy's nothing but a pawn," he said. "Why do I have to look after him?"

That voice was more of a whine than anything, but it was definitely male.

"Because you're being well paid."

"You could keep him here," he said. "Nobody would know."

"I would know," the first voice said in a hard tone. "You know how we get the cops in here every once in a while. What if they came in and found the prisoner here?"

"Well, you could just let him free," he said. "It's not like he did anything wrong."

"He's bait. How hard is that for you to figure out?" he said. "Also, if you keep talking, you'll just piss me off further, and I'll decide I don't want to listen to your voice anymore and will just cut off your tongue."

Immediately there was silence, perhaps meaning that the other guy firmly believed the threat to be exactly what would happen. Kano and Garret shifted slightly, so they were directly underneath the voices, trying to peer through the floorboards, but they found no way to see who was talking. Garret figured the tongue-cutting guy to be the owner of the bar, the father tied to one of Kingdom's men.

"We do need to find where the girlfriend disappeared to though."

"Why? Who even cares about her?"

"We won't leave any threads hanging, dumbass," he said. "If this job doesn't go the way we think it'll go, then we have to dispose of the evidence. All the evidence, including her."

At that, the other man gasped. "She's pregnant. You know that, right? We can't off a pregnant woman. That's just wrong."

"Yeah, so what do you want to do about it?" the first guy said.

There was silence once again. "We could just let her go. She doesn't know nothing."

"But we know," he said. "And if we know, she knows."

That obviously confused the other man because more silence came.

With Kano and Garret obviously in the right place, yet not knowing where the hell his brother was, they didn't want to move, in case somebody set something off.

"You need to get the hell out of here and don't come back. I don't want to bother with you."

"I get it," he said. "I won't be back. I promise." And, with that, he dashed out.

Immediately Kano took off, hoping to come around and find this gopher guy. Garret and Kano had been texting madly with Charles to see if he could find out who this guy was, but the chances of that happening weren't good. Being the only one now under the floorboards, Garret listened intently, hearing the orders that, as he'd expected, were given to another man.

"Go take care of him now, will you? Also, while you're at it, we'll have to move the prisoner."

"Yeah, where do you want to keep him?"

"Well, I'd say here, but I don't want to bring it so close to home. What other location do we have?"

"We could move him to Maggie's place?"

"Yes, let's do that. She won't be happy, but I don't care.

Take him to Maggie's place."

"Well, if we take care of this whiny guy, is there any reason we can't just leave our prisoner where he is?"

"Unless the cops come and look into it. And they go to his place to investigate for sure."

There was more silence, as the men mulled things over.

"Sounds like Maggie's place is it," the one guy said.

"You know that she's got a big mouth though," the other one warned. "But she's got that big apartment over her garage. It's got a separate entrance. What if we don't even tell her?"

The two men thought about that, tossed up a few arguments for and against it, and then one guy said, "I'll do it, and we can always pay her off, if we need to."

"Yeah, true enough. She'll do anything for money." And they both sniggered. The second man got up and left. What Garret needed desperately was to find a way to see these guys, to figure out their identities. Also, who the hell was this Maggie? She was about to host his brother as an uninvited guest.

Moving, he tripped a little and accidentally kicked a small rock that he hadn't seen. Immediately the man above jumped to his feet and called out, "Who's there?"

Garret ducked down in the darkness.

"Is anybody there?"

"Barnie, come here," the man called. Immediately another man came running. "Go down to the basement. You know the alcove, directly under here? Check and see who's down there." As Barnie went to run away, he said, "Go armed, and make sure nobody comes out of there alive."

Swearing to himself, Garret slipped back out, headed to the basement, and on to the alleyway. He barely got clear and slipped behind the dumpster, when another man burst from the same grate.

The gunman looked around and pulled out his phone. "Boss, I can't see anyone. ... Oh, yeah, no. I'll check again. ... Yeah, I know. I'm sure. ... Yeah, sure, I'll check again." He went back down again through the grate, swearing.

As soon as he was gone, Garret came out and texted Kano. **Where are you?**

Out front. And I got a license plate on the one guy's vehicle.

Good. We need to go. They'll move my brother ... tonight.

CHAPTER 8

ASTRA STARED AT the text that just came in, shocked. She leaned over and held it up for Charles to see.

He looked at it, smiled, and said, "My dear, that's very good news, indeed."

"Is it?" she said in a shaken whisper. "Though it doesn't sound like it's a done deal."

"No, but we've shaken something loose, and that's good."

"But have we shaken something even looser?"

"Doesn't matter," he said, as he looked at her beer. "Drink up, my dear. It looks like we need to move." She picked up the glass, tilted it back, and guzzled it. When she put it down again and wiped her lips, he grinned and said, "There's something very sexy about a woman drinking a beer like that."

She chuckled. "Sorry, I'm taken."

"Oh, I know, dear," he said, as he hopped out of the booth, lifted his arm to her, and said, "May I?" With a grace that she wasn't expecting, and the charm that she had already seen twinkling through, he patted her hand, as he tucked it through his elbow and said, "Believe me. It's very obvious, to anybody who cares to look."

"I was hoping it wasn't," she wailed. "We're definitely not in a relationship."

"Oh, you are," he said. "You're just still doing the dance that's as old as time, and nobody's quite ready to get to the point yet."

"It's not that nobody's ready," she said in a dry tone. "It's just that it's complicated, and we've barely had two minutes to ourselves."

"Very valid point," he said, with a bright smile. "Hopefully, when this mess is all over ..."

"Exactly, but I don't know what that'll take," she said.

"Well, with any luck, tonight we'll find his brother," he said. As they walked out and headed toward the car, it came racing toward them, driven by Garret, Kano already in the passenger seat.

"Hop in," Garret said, his tone curt.

They immediately scrambled in, as he took off down the road.

"Where to?" Astra asked.

"To Maggie's place," Garret said, "whatever and whoever Maggie is. I've got my team on it."

Charles looked at him and said, "*Hmm*, the barmaid who served us was called Maggie."

"Was that her name?" Astra asked, looking at Charles.

"That's what her name tag said."

Garret pulled over, grabbed his phone, and very quickly said, "I have her address." As he peeled out again, picking up speed, Kano punched the numbers into the navigation app, while he started his own search.

"I'll run the license number." A moment later, Kano said, "Got it," reading the name of the whiny guy. "He's the one who took off with orders to keep looking after Gregg."

"Interesting," Charles said. "He's a local lowlife."

"He is, and he's being used in this case as well," Garret

added, "but what he doesn't realize yet is that orders have been given to deal with him tonight. Permanently."

"Oh, dear," Charles said. "That's never good news."

Astra sat back and watched as the men spoke in this half language they all seemed to be fluent in, but she was not. She understood enough to get the gist but not the details. Apparently the person who had been looking after Gregg until now was causing some sort of trouble and would be taken out of the equation. Gregg would get moved, and Maggie, whether she knew it or not, was about to become Gregg's new landlord. "So can we go to Maggie's?" Astra asked.

"Well, we really should step in earlier than that," Charles said apologetically. "We can hardly allow the one guy to be murdered."

"Right," she said suddenly.

"That would be unfortunate, and he couldn't supply much information dead, could he?" Kano laughed.

"I like the way you think," Garret said. "It's definitely refreshing to know that somebody doesn't waste much time on the ugly side of life."

"There's no point," she said. "When you think about it, that guy has already made his choice. He walked outside of a normal life, a long time ago. For all we know, he's the one who kidnapped your brother."

"Maybe," he said. "Although he won't do it twice."

"Exactly," she said, with a smile.

As they turned a corner, the GPS told them they were there. Garret turned to look at the buildings in front of them and all around. "You two stay here," Garret said. "Kano and I will take a look around."

They hopped out and disappeared, as she sank back in

the seat and murmured, "They do that a lot."

"Taking off on you?"

She nodded and smiled at him.

"It's the business," he said. "It really can't be helped."

Very quickly Astra saw them slide up to the front door of the target address. They knocked, but they got no answer. No vehicles were here either. "Do you think the bad guys waylaid this one on his way home?"

"Or maybe he stopped for a drink somewhere," Charles said.

Right. As the two men at the front door eased it open, she asked, "Is this safe?"

"No," he said. "It definitely is not."

The men went in, and she waited on tenterhooks, until Charles reached over, patted her arm gently, and said, "It may not be safe, but these are men who do this work, day in and day out."

"It's not an easy life," she murmured.

"No, but that's something you need to realize, since that's the kind of life you would be joining."

She thought about that and nodded. "I guess that's the difference between me and my sister. She wanted his brother to quit."

"Pregnancy could be a part of that too," he said.

"I know. She doesn't like me mentioning it all the time, but it's true."

"Yes," he said. "I get that. It's hard though, isn't it?"

She nodded in agreement and said, "It is hard to watch somebody you love going through a situation like that."

"Why do I get the impression that you have loved him for a very long time?" he asked.

"Because I have. Ever since Amy brought Garret home

that very first time. I knew it was wrong and that I couldn't do anything about it, so I just buried myself in my work." She laughed. "It actually turned out to be a good thing because we've helped put a lot of criminals behind bars and have found a lot of children and young women, releasing them from the purgatory they suffered in. I'm good at what I do, but I would definitely like to see life open to include Garret in some way."

"No reason it can't. You both need to understand that the kind of work you do is dark, definitely dangerous, and profoundly unpleasant. Even if it's not physically dangerous, it's dangerous in the sense of your mental health. So, as much as you'll have to deal with what he comes home with, he will also have to deal with what you bring home."

She gave Charles a smile and said, "Then neither of us are a good bet."

"It doesn't matter," he said. "So long as you're betting on each other, you'll be fine."

She chuckled at that. "Well, we're a long way from anything like that."

"Not as long as you may think," he said, then motioned out the car window. "Look. They're already coming out."

She stared in surprise. "Oh, that means Gregg's not here, damn it," she said, as both of the men slipped into the car.

"The house is empty," Garret said.

"I'm tracking his vehicle," Charles said, holding up his phone. "It's parked outside another pub," he added, then quickly gave them the address.

"Do you think the courier's still alive?" Astra asked anybody in the car.

"I don't know," Garret said, "but what I do know is that my brother's not being held here."

"So the courier guy's got another place," she said. "Maybe we'd be better off staking out Maggie's house, until they move Gregg."

"Check the pub first," Charles said. "Let's make sure this gopher guy is even still alive, and then we'll have to set up a stakeout at Maggie's."

"Not much fun," she said.

"None of it is fun," Garret said, "but it's what we have to do. We're close, really close, so let's not screw it up now."

"No," she murmured. "I get it." Just then her phone rang, and it was her sister. "No, I don't know anything yet, and we are getting closer, yes."

"Where are you?" Amy said, in tears. "I don't want to be here alone."

"Maybe not, but you're safe there," she said to her sister. At that, Amy started to cry again. "Look. We'll be home soon," she said, desperately trying to ward off a big scene. At that, her sister hung up. Astra sagged back in her seat and said, "I sure hope we find him soon."

"I do too," Garret said. "But did you ever consider that finding him may not result in the return of somebody who she thinks she wants?"

"Meaning, that he may not want to go back? Is that what you mean?" Astra asked.

"It's definitely something we have to consider."

"Well, I'll consider it, if and when it happens," she said. "When we find him, and he tells me that he'll walk away from his responsibilities."

"That's not what I'm saying," Garret replied. "He'll end up being part of the child's life. I can't see him doing anything but that. However, that's no guarantee he wants to have a life with Amy."

"And I think that would be devastating for her," she murmured.

"Maybe so," he said, "but it's something we have to consider."

"I hope not," she said. "I'm not sure she could handle that."

"We can handle far more than we're aware of," Charles said, with a smile.

"Maybe," Astra said, "but my sister isn't terribly willing to try. She wants the white picket fence, attentive husband, and three perfect kids."

"And maybe she'll get it," Charles said. "We still have to believe in hope, in romance."

"I'd like to just believe in happy," she said, with half a smile. Before she realized it, they were pulling up to the second pub. "Are we going in to have another pint?" she asked Charles.

He looked at her and smiled. "Would you like one?"

"Oh, yes," she said. "I'd love another one. Besides, these two guys aren't dressed for it. We can go in and see if he's there, at least."

"I'll go check out his vehicle," Garret said.

They all got out and proceeded with their various assignments. When Astra and Charles were seated at the bar, each with a tall pint in front of them, she looked at hers and smiled. "I have to say that I really love the color."

"These are both particularly pale ambers," he said. "I usually prefer a good stout myself."

She chuckled. "Not me," she said. "I'm glad that you ordered a pale amber too. Don't worry. If you can't drink that, I will."

His gaze widened, and she nodded, smiling. "I know.

Most women don't like beer, but that's crap. I really enjoy a good beer myself."

"Glad to hear it," he said, as he pushed his over to her. "Because I won't enjoy this one."

She smiled, and, as soon as she had hers gone, she picked up his and turned to look around. "Have we heard from them?"

"No," he said. "Not yet."

She nodded. "Oh, that's too bad."

"What is?" he asked.

"They're at the door, waving at us. And I've got this beautiful beer here."

His gaze twinkled. She looked at him, looked at the beer, and said, "What the hell." With that, she picked it up and threw it back. When she slammed down the glass, she gave him a grin and said, "Let's roll."

"Next stop?"

"Let's hope it's another pub," she said, giggling.

Laughing and thoroughly enjoying himself, Charles escorted her to the front door, the two of them snickering like children.

Garret looked at her and said, "Did you just guzzle both pints?"

"No, not at all," she said, trying for a straight face. "Why would you think that?"

"It's what I saw," he said.

"I don't think 'guzzle' is the word I would use. Charles?"

"Never, my dear. *Chug* perhaps."

That sent her into a fit of giggles and left Garret shaking his head.

When they were back in the vehicle, however, she was all business. "So, what's going on?"

"We found the courier."

"And?"

"He's dead."

"Where is he?" she asked, her voice sober.

"In the trunk of his car." He twisted in the seat to look at Charles. "You want to call Jonas?"

"Of course," he said, and moments later they heard Charles making the report to MI6. Garret sat back against the front seat, his face grim, as he mapped out a route to Maggie's house. He showed it to Kano, who nodded. The trip was hard and fast, but the silence in the back seat worried him the most. He twisted to look back at her. She had a pinched gray look to her face. "You okay, Astra?"

She gave him a soft look and said, "Yes, I was on a nice buzz from the beer, but that news was enough to send anybody's good cheer down the drain."

"It is," he said. "I wish you were back at Charles' place, with your sister."

She gave him a ghost of a smile. "That wasn't part of the plan."

"No, it wasn't part of the plan, at least not part of your plan," he said. "But it certainly would be nice for my plan."

"Not happening," she said, chuckling.

He shook his head. "Just saying, that's all."

"Maybe so, but it's not happening, so don't worry about it."

"What do you want to do then? The next place could be bad."

"It can't all be bad," she said. "I'm here. Charles's here. We'll hold down the fort, as you guys do what you need to do."

He hesitated, and she reached her hand over the seat,

closer to him. Garret immediately grabbed it and hung on.

"We'll find him," she said gently.

He squeezed her fingers and said, "I know. We definitely will. The question is, what shape will he be in?"

She winced at that. "We'll hold on to the belief that he'll be alive and fine, once he's out of there."

"Okay."

She smiled. "Come on. We'll make it through this."

"We will."

She stopped, then not giving herself the chance to bite back the words, she said, "I'm living in New York these days."

"New York?" he said, with a raised eyebrow. "I thought you said France?"

"No, I was at a conference in France, when I last saw Amy," Astra said. "I do travel a lot. That might be a problem."

He gave half a snort. "I do a lot of traveling too."

"New York is easy to get in and out of at least," she said.

He glanced at her, and a smile was in his gaze. "Is this leading somewhere?"

Yes," she said, carrying on bravely. "I thought maybe you'd like to go for coffee sometime?"

He chuckled. "If you're asking me out on a date, the answer is definitely yes."

She chuckled too. "Well, I'm still a bit old-fashioned and figured you should do the asking, but I thought coffee was safe."

"How about we go out for dinner when we meet up in New York?"

"Is that a nebulous if and when?" she asked.

"Not necessarily," he said. "When this nightmare is over.

How's that?"

"That is a definite possibility," she said, and she let his fingers go.

"The other thing is," he said, "since we both travel a lot, we could meet up in other places too."

"I'd like that," she said, settling back comfortably. "I'm due for a holiday in London."

"Why London?" he asked.

"Because I like London," she said, "and I'm still dealing with some family stuff."

"We could both be dealing with a lot of family stuff after this," he said. "There's not just my brother but also your sister to consider."

"Who could ever forget," she said, laughing.

"It is what it is," he said.

"I know."

Just then Charles got off the phone, and the vehicle rolled to a stop. With both those things happening so suddenly, she looked around and asked, "Is this Maggie's house?"

With no lights on in the car, they remained inside the vehicle, parked a couple houses from what looked like was probably the house where Maggie lived because it was the only one nearby with a garage.

"Supposed to be a space above the garage," he said.

She pointed. "There?"

"That's what our GPS is saying," Kano said. "And it's got the only garage in sight." He looked at Garret. "We could be early."

"I suggest we scope it out first," Garret said, then looked back at Charles.

Charles smiled, patted Astra's arm, and said, "We'll sit

here and wait."

The men got out, walked down the street together, quickly disappearing from sight.

She sagged back against the seat. "How did I do?"

"I think you did brilliantly," he said. "When you think about it, you haven't had a whole lot of opportunity to get anything out there, so today was lovely."

"It felt pushy," she muttered.

"Guys like Garret, they don't normally jump in. Especially in this case because of all the family stuff going on. In such a circumstance, a little pushiness may be required."

"That's what I thought," she said.

"It was well done," he said. "You'll probably have to fine-tune it a bit though."

"Yeah, he'll leave it as nebulous, won't he?"

"He might," Charles said, with a chuckle. "But if he's smart, he won't ..." and he let his voice trail off.

She smiled, settled back, and said, "No, he won't be smart about it at all."

"In that case," Charles said, "you might want to up your game a little bit."

She chuckled. "Not sure I know how to do that."

"You don't have to think about it, don't rationalize it," he said. "Just do what comes naturally."

"I'll have to think about that," she said, as she yawned. "You know what? Sitting in a warm vehicle after all that beer, I'm about to crash."

"Close your eyes," he said. "It's all good."

"Says you. I'm not used to sleeping in a vehicle like this."

"You're also not used to being in a vehicle on a stakeout," he said. "These things can be long and drawn out, so enjoy yourself while you can."

"Not sure how much of this is enjoyment, but—"

"Stop," he said. "Close your eyes, and get some rest. It's all good."

She chuckled and said, "Are you always this forceful?"

"Always," he said. "Now rest."

GARRET, WITH KANO at his side, did a quick visual on the outside of the house—no lights were on, no sign anybody was home, and no vehicles in the garage. They tested the front door and found it locked. They slipped around to the back. It was also locked, but the kitchen window was wide open. He always wondered at people who locked the doors but left everything else wide open and accessible.

Pushing the window fully open, Kano slipped inside, Garret right behind him. They spread out, scoping out the left and right side of the house on the main floor, finding nothing. They slipped downstairs, again nothing. The basement was completely empty. In a way that was nice because they didn't have to worry about somebody hiding among the boxes and relics of a time gone by that so many basements were full of. When he got back to the main floor, he pointed upward, and they scooted up the stairs, but again the place was empty.

He stared at the space over the garage and said, "So that's our goal." At least no one else was here for them to contend with.

Back out of the house Garret slowly lowered the kitchen window down to precisely where it had been open before, and they moved quietly through the darkness to the garage. Inside the garage, they checked for an interior entrance and exit to the upstairs but there wasn't one. Back outside they found a set of steps with a bit of a covering overhead to keep it dry from the moisture, and they quickly moved their way up to the entrance. It wasn't in great shape, definitely not to code, but that was typical of a lot of these places. He had the door unlocked in seconds.

Going on instincts, Garret pushed open the door, then kept to the back. Inside, he heard movement, but nothing that made a cry, no bullet, or anything that suggested danger. It could be mice, for all he knew. A sound that small, more of a scurrying noise.

With Kano's gaze hard, the two of them pulled out the weapons that Charles had supplied and entered slowly.

They followed along a single long space with a bedroom at the very end, and, from the looks of it, a bathroom, kitchenette, and living room. It all appeared to be empty. Garret moved slowly through the space, avoiding the windows, in case anybody approached. This was the point in time when they could easily get caught.

Kano came up behind him and said, "It's empty."

"It appears to be, yes," he said.

"I don't like the fact that there's only one entrance. If we get caught in here, we're screwed." They immediately turned and headed toward the steps. As they did so, headlights came up the street.

Garret swore and said, "New arrivals are here."

"The good news," Kano said, "is that your brother could be in that vehicle." They barely made their way down the steps before they heard a single set of footsteps coming toward them. Making a quick decision, Garret grabbed Kano and pulled him into the trees. The two watched as someone slithered around the corner and up the steps, quickly looking around the area to make sure he wasn't being seen. But he came alone.

Garret and Kano checked out the new guy's vehicle, parked on the far side of the road. Garret texted Charles, who confirmed he already had the license plate and was searching it. Garret held up his phone to show Kano, as the new man came back out the door and quickly slipped back down the steps again.

He was already on his phone. "It's empty. Nobody here. It's perfect timing. ... Yeah, yeah, I know. I'll get him here soon." With that, he raced out to his vehicle.

Kano and Garret had slipped behind the nearest bushes, then after the new guy pulled away, hopped into their vehicle, and tore out after him, trying to find out where his brother was being stashed.

Charles asked, "Is that him?"

"He was talking to his boss about moving someone," Garret said. "I can only hope it's my brother."

"God, I hope it's him," Astra said. "Imagine if they are holding somebody else."

He turned to look at her. "I thought you were asleep."

"I was," she said, "until we took off like a jet engine."

He chuckled. "Well, the good news is, we're on the tail of the person who's supposed to be delivering someone here."

"So why didn't we just wait there?" she asked in a reasonable tone of voice.

"That was one option," he said.

Charles piped up then. "Jonas is coming in with somebody to watch the place," he said in an almost apologetic tone of voice.

"Great," Kano said. "All we need is MI6 interference."

"Let's hope it's not interference," she said, "and look at it as backup instead."

Both men shot her a look and shook their heads, returning their attention to the road ahead. The other vehicle didn't drive for very long and didn't appear to notice they had a tail. Garret presumed it was because he was spooked about what his job was. As the guy pulled into a driveway, he turned the vehicle around, as if to load something. They pulled up past the house and turned around, then killed the lights and pulled up on the side. Immediately Garret and Kano shifted out of the vehicle and raced off into the darkness.

CHAPTER 9

A S SOON AS Garret and Kano returned to the car, Astra leaned forward and asked, "What did you find?"

"We found an empty apartment, and somebody who had just arrived, heading up there. He was on his phone, talking about bringing somebody. Hopefully they're bringing my brother."

"So now what?" she asked, and she could hardly control the excitement in her voice.

"You, nothing." Garret said. He turned back to look at Charles.

Charles just shrugged. "Sure, we could have stayed home," he said. "But I have to admit, a little bit of fieldwork is good for me too."

At that, Kano laughed. "You get plenty of fieldwork, and it all comes through your house."

"Maybe," he said cheerfully, "but I'll never say no to the company of a lovely lady. I like to have things operate out of my own sphere," he said, "but we've enjoyed a couple lovely little pubs."

"And I got to drink some of his beer," she said.

Garret turned and looked at her in surprise. "I knew it. What is it with you and the beer?"

She shrugged. "What can I say? I like a good brew."

Garret flashed a grin at her, and then Kano whispered,

"They've got company."

At that, silence fell in their vehicle, and they all were focused on what they might see and hear. She watched as another vehicle pulled up behind the first one. "I wonder if Gregg is in there."

As they watched, two men got out and headed toward the vehicle. As they approached, the two men in the first vehicle got out as well. There seemed to be some sort of conflict going on; then one of the men in the second vehicle pulled out a handgun, fired several shots and killed both of the men from the first vehicle.

She gasped in shock. "Oh, my God. Oh, my God," she whispered.

Charles reached over and gently patted her hand. She looked at him. The men, although their faces were grim and dark, didn't appear to be all that surprised.

She said, "If Gregg's in that car—"

"If he's in that car," he said, "believe me, they're not taking him. But we don't know yet that he's actually in that vehicle."

"But weren't they supposed to bring him?"

"Yes," he said, "somebody was to bring someone. But that doesn't mean this is the same group. We may be dealing with a separate group here."

"I don't like all this secret spy stuff," she said mutinously.

Charles gave a chuckle. "For somebody who doesn't like it, you've spent quite a lot of time in the industry."

"Sure, but behind the scenes," she said. "I don't have to deal with this stuff, person to person."

"It's good for everyone to deal with it like this, to some degree," Charles said. "You really don't understand what's going on in the world, until you see it at this level."

She had to agree with him, but she didn't like it. As she watched, the two men who had killed the other two now turned, looked up at the apartment, had a discussion, and then made their way into the apartment, as if to check it out themselves. And, as soon as that happened, both Kano and Garret, without a word, silently opened their doors and disappeared.

She looked at Charles. "Now where are they going?"

"To check out the contents of the two vehicles," he said.

She sagged back in relief. "Oh, that makes sense," she said. "I just ... I'm not used to thinking along those lines."

"Nobody does," he said, with a gentle smile. "It's not a life that any of us particularly want to have access to or to get used to."

"So true," she murmured. She watched as the men went to the first vehicle, bent down over the two men on the ground, and, when that obviously didn't interest them, she presumed that they were both dead. Garret opened the driver's seat and pulled the lever to release the trunk. Kano was already there; he lifted it up, said something to Garret, and they closed it.

"Oh no, oh no," she said. "He's not in there. They checked inside the vehicle, but there was nothing. So now what?"

"I don't know," Charles said in a worried tone.

"And what if somebody else comes?" she said.

"We'll have to see," he said.

"I didn't even know you gave them handguns," she said.

"I didn't want them to come out without weapons," he said, "and you can see why."

She did see why; she just didn't like anything about it.

The two suddenly disappeared into the trees, and she understood a moment later, as the two killers were coming back.

"It's like watching a horror movie," she said, "without any guarantee that you'll like the ending."

Charles chuckled. "That's a good way to look at it," he said. "This is action all the way."

"Still pretty stressful," she muttered.

"Definitely stressful."

As they watched, the two killers got into their vehicle and started it up. Charles got out of the back seat, stepped into the front seat, and turned on the engine. The vehicle drove past slowly. Charles completely ignored them as they drove away. He prepared to pull out, turned the vehicle around, and Kano and Garret both got in. Just like that, Charles was now the driver. And he gunned it, taking off after the other two men.

"Is this safe?" Astra asked.

"Maybe not," Garret said, "but we can't take any chances on losing them."

"Why would they kill the other two men like that?"

"I'm speculating here, but I think that somebody else is after my brother. Either after him or has a better use for him."

"Oh, my God," she whispered and sank against the back seat. Garret was beside her with Kano in the front with Charles. Garret reached over, snagged her up, and pulled her in tight against him.

"We're working on this," he said. "We'll find my brother."

She nodded slowly. "I don't doubt that," she said. "I'm just a little concerned about what I'm supposed to—with what happens in the meantime."

"We'll find him. And we have to trust that he's alive and that he's somewhere nearby."

She nodded. "This is really a cat-and-mouse game, isn't it?"

"It is, indeed."

She gave a heavy sigh and sank against him. He tucked her up even closer and murmured against her hair, "I promise we're doing everything that we can."

She nodded. "I know," she whispered. "I'm just really glad my sister isn't here."

"I am too," he said. Just then somebody's phone went off.

She looked around, but it was coming from the front seat. "Charles, is that your phone?"

"It is, indeed." He tossed it to Kano, giving him a number to unlock the phone.

Kano said, "It's your house."

With that, Charles gave him another number to dial into the security system.

Kano was reading now. "According to the printout, the front door's been opened."

At that, Charles's gaze shifted, looking at Kano in surprise.

"From the inside," he said grimly.

"Amy," Astra cried out. "Damn it."

"Yes, Amy has left the building."

"Why would she do that?" Astra asked. "I thought we left her leashed inside."

"Unfortunately it was always a possibility," Charles said.

At his tone of voice, she sank back, looked at him, and asked, "In what way?" Nobody wanted to say it outright. She turned and looked at Garret head-on. "You expect my sister is a part of this?"

"We're not sure what we're expecting, but Charles left the door available as an option to see what she'd do," he said. "But she needs to have a damn good reason why she left secure surroundings."

"How about the fact that we left her alone?" she said.

"And why is that?" he said, sending her a hard look.

She shrugged. "Because I didn't want to be left behind. I wanted to be out here, to see what was going on. Besides, it was good for Charles to have somebody here."

"Yes," Garret said, "but it was also good to have you at home, with her."

"If you're thinking that I could have kept her in the house, I think you're wrong."

"Really?" Charles asked.

"Yeah, my sister's always been the one to do things her way."

Garret thought about that for a long moment, then nodded. "Good point," he said. He looked at Charles. "Do you have any way to track her, once she's left ... left the building?"

"Yes," he said, "at least for a little bit." He added, "I wish I could set it in motion."

"Tell me," Kano said. "Just walk me through it." After a little bit of difficulty and backtracking, finally he managed to get it set up.

"Where is she?" Garret asked.

"Heading down the street, completely unconcerned."

"Can you see her now?" Astra asked.

"The video's old," Kano said, "as in a few minutes ago. I'm not seeing her in real time, but probably a ten-minute delay."

"Ten minutes is not very much," she muttered.

"No, it's not," Kano said. "Now it looks like she's stopped and is flagging down a vehicle. Unfortunately it looks like she knows whoever it is because she just waved and got in."

"Shit," Astra said, sinking back. What was her sister up to? She knew better than to get into a vehicle with a stranger. But the alternative scared the crap out of Astra.

"Okay, Astra, listen to me carefully," Garret said. "So I know she's your sister, and I know you love her, but … do you trust her?"

She was in a daze, when she turned to look at Garret. "I guess you're asking if she could be a part of this. I would never have thought so before, but I don't know how to explain her actions."

"Neither do I, but that doesn't mean there isn't an explanation," he said.

"I figured you'd be the first one to believe the worst of her."

"Maybe," he said, "but I'm not sure that applies in this case. She's young and irresponsible, and she really wants him out of the industry. What lengths would she go to, to make it so that he wanted out as well?"

She stared at him. "Please tell me that you don't think she staged the whole kidnapping, just to teach him a lesson?"

"I don't know what to think," he said. "And it has us completely sidetracked from something pretty important."

"I'm sorry," she murmured. "You're right. It has, hasn't it?"

"Yes. So I dearly hope it's not all in vain."

"I would hope not," Charles said. "I know I keep bringing this up, but pregnant women—"

"It had damn well better not be because of that," she murmured in a hard voice. "That gets old very quickly."

"Yes," Charles said, "for all of us."

GARRET DIDN'T KNOW what to tell Astra; he had no real way to reassure her because this was a really worrisome addition to their situation. "It's also possible," he said, "that Amy might have just called an old friend and decided to spend the evening out."

"Yeah, she would do that too," Astra muttered, staring out the window. "She doesn't really see much around her, other than herself."

"And she also knows that evenings out are a diminishing resource for her, and something she won't maintain since she is pregnant," he said quietly. "At some point, she'll need to stay home with a baby."

"Yeah, I don't think anybody bothered to tell her that," she muttered.

"But she wants the baby, correct?"

"Yes," she nodded. "Definitely."

"So then we have to trust that she won't do anything that'll put the baby at risk."

She nodded. "And again, I hear you. I just don't like this new development." At that, she realized that the vehicle was still going strong. She leaned forward and asked, "Do we have any idea where this guy is going?"

"No, not really," Charles said. "I mean, he's heading back toward the center of London. That can mean all kinds of things."

"And how do you avoid having him see you?"

"That's a good question," he said. "So far, he's not show-ing any signs of suspecting somebody's on him. But then again," he added, with a bright smile, "he's not really paying attention. He's on the phone."

"Well, that's good. Any distraction for him is good for us," Garret said.

She agreed. "What if I call my sister?" she asked.

"Go for it," Garret said. "Play dumb, and see if she tells you where she is."

Realizing it would probably be another test of some sort, she sank back and called her sister, putting it on Speaker-phone. Garret couldn't hear all of the conversation, but he heard enough.

"I couldn't stay in the house," she said. "I'm bored to tears. You guys left me alone to go on some stupid wild goose chase. Why should I have to sit there all by myself?"

"Well, you were supposed to be resting," Astra said.

"All I've done is rest," she said resentfully. "It's my life that's all mixed up here, you know?"

"Absolutely. So who did you call to spend time with for the evening then?"

"What makes you think I called anybody?"

"I can't imagine you going out alone. Not being preg-nant."

"You keep harping on me being pregnant," she said. "Why is that any different now?"

"Because I was thinking you would never put your baby in danger," she said, "or am I wrong?"

"Of course not," she said, "but just going out for an evening. That can't possibly hurt."

"Which is why I'm pretty sure you're not alone," she said. "So do you mind telling me who you're with?"

"An old friend," she said cagily.

"What kind of an old friend?"

"Somebody Gregg used to work with," she said.

Instantly the other men turned to look at her.

She said, "Then you won't mind telling me his name."

"I won't tell you his name because you're acting like I've done something wrong," she said, her voice turning petulant.

"Oh, for crying out loud. I just want to know that you're safe," she said. "How is that so difficult to understand?"

At that, her sister sniffed. "I'm not at all sure," she said, "that's what this is all about. When are you coming back anyway?"

"Soon," she said, with a shrug at Garret and Kano.

They just nodded.

"So you say," Amy said. "that could mean anything. I won't sit in the house by myself all evening."

"Fine, so who are you with then?" In the background she heard a man telling Amy to shut off the phone.

"I'm not shutting off the phone," she said. "It's my sister."

"Even better," the man said. "Hang up the phone."

"No, I already told you that I'm not hanging up. Just keep driving. I need a drink."

"You're not drinking with the baby, are you?" Astra asked.

"Oh, for God's sake, give me a break," she said. "Just because I want something to drink, doesn't mean it can't be coffee."

"That's true," Astra said, with half a smile. She looked at the other two men, as if asking what to say. "So you'll be at a pub then?"

"And again, there you are with the questions."

"Well, so far you haven't answered any, so you can't blame a girl for trying," she said. "And you're going out of your way, trying to piss me off by evading the simplest questions, which is very suspicious."

"Hang up the phone," said the man.

"No, I'm not. My sister might be nosy, but she's harmless."

"Yeah, I'm harmless," she said, "unless I think you're in trouble."

"I'm not in trouble," she said. "I've spent lots of time with this guy. Haven't I, Rick?"

"Don't call me by my name, and hang up the damn phone."

Astra heard a struggle going on, with her sister crying out. Finally Amy got her phone back and said, "I have to hang up now." But she was sobbing, and, all of a sudden, the phone went dead. Astra put hers down very carefully and said, "Oh, my God."

"What?"

"I think she's in trouble."

The vehicle in front of them picked up speed and ripped around a corner, hard.

CHAPTER 10

A STRA WAS FLUNG from one side to the next, as Charles chased after the vehicle in front.

Garret reached out, snatched her into his arms, and held her close, using his legs to brace them, as they went around corners.

"Is my sister involved in this?"

"I'm not sure," he said, "but it's possible. Do you know who this Rick person is?"

"I think she mentioned him before, somebody who Gregg worked with."

"That's what she said, but is he a good guy or not a good guy?"

"As far as I remember, he kept asking Gregg to go work for him."

"Privately?"

"Yeah, but I don't know what the job was."

"It's probably something off the books too."

"I don't know what that means, but it doesn't sound good."

"No," Garret said, "I doubt that it is. But we can't jump to conclusions. I just know from the sound of what we heard that, whatever scenario your sister has gotten herself into, it doesn't look good."

Just then the vehicle ahead whipped into a car park.

Garret himself almost missed it. Just as the taillights went around, he caught it. Immediately Charles turned into the same place and blocked the side entrance. Garret slipped out, and so did Kano. She watched in shock, as they disappeared. She leaned forward to the front seat and asked Charles, "Do we just sit here, in the middle of the road?"

"No," he said. "I'll take this parking spot, right up here," and he pulled the large vehicle in and around, moving it quietly into the back corner.

She asked, "Now what?" She watched as Charles pulled a handgun from the glove box. "Now we wait again," he said.

"I don't feel so good about my sister right now."

"No," he said, "neither do I. We're trying to get a make on the vehicle she got into and to see if we can get an alert sent out on it."

"I still don't understand why she would have left to go with him in the first place."

"She obviously knew him," he said. "The question is, how well did she know him?"

"And how did he get her to leave?"

"I don't know," Charles said. "That's something you might answer, but, for us, it's hard to know. It was enough for her to walk out of the safety of my house though."

"Who would know that she'd gone in there?"

"Somebody who was monitoring Kano's and Garret's calls or movements. Or she got a call and told them where she was."

"But going to your place was all very secret."

"True, but a lot of people in that world know the business I'm in," he said quietly. "It's one of the reasons I keep extra safeguards in place, so that we are secure in there. But, once you leave it, you're out in the big bad world again."

"Damn," she said, settling back. "Amy's always been one to do things her own way."

"Do you think there's any chance that the baby isn't Gregg's?"

"That would be sad," she said. "I can't really tell you the answer to that."

"And you don't have to," he said. "We can only hope that we get answers sooner than later."

"It's just really suspicious that she left at the same time we're out looking for Gregg."

There was a commotion, and, even from where they were parked, the sounds came through the vehicle. She gasped and leaned forward, pointing. "There. What was that?"

Charles hesitated.

"Shouldn't we go help them?"

"No," he said. "There are times when you have to trust in their abilities, and this is one of them."

"But, if I wasn't here, you would go, wouldn't you?"

He nodded. "Well, yes," he said reluctantly. "I would, indeed."

"Then go," she said. "Unlike my sister, I know to stay put."

He hesitated.

She said, "No, don't hesitate because of me. Just go. We have to make sure that nobody else gets hurt because of this mess. I'm already afraid my sister is involved to a point that—that she's hurting the people I care about."

He looked back at her and said, "They'll be fine."

"But you don't even believe that yourself. You don't know what they're up against." She added, "Would it be so terrible to go as a backup, just in case? Everybody needs help at one time or another."

He chuckled at that. "Very true," he said. "You have to promise."

"I promise," she said. Maybe her reaction was a little too fast because he looked at her. "I promise," she said again. "I won't do anything stupid."

"Says you," he said, but he got up and headed outside with one final look. "Please stay in place." She nodded. And, with that, he was gone. She watched what was going on outside, feeling helpless and useless. She quickly dialed her sister back, and, when there was no answer, she sent a text.

Her sister responded. **I think I'm in trouble**.

Astra groaned. **Rick?**

Yes, he's not who I thought he was.

And she wasn't at all surprised. **Where are you?**

I need a ride. I'm in trouble.

Where are you, Amy?

Come and get me.

But her sister was not making any sense and not giving her any directions.

Where are you? Tell me so I can help.

And then there was nothing. Astra groaned and bent her head over her knees, wondering who the hell she could call for help. This night had seriously gone to shit. When her phone buzzed suddenly, she was surprised but delighted to see it was her sister again. But the message was one that immediately had her blood boiling.

We have your sister. We'll trade her for her boyfriend.

Just then, two more vehicles came in the car park behind her. As she watched, they whipped around at a speed that was not normal at all. Still in shock from the message she had just received, she sat here, watching, as they headed around to where the men had disappeared from. Now she realized she was up against an ugly choice. Did she listen to Charles and stay in place? Or did she go see if she could help them get out of trouble?

She quickly sent a message to Garret, telling him that two vehicles full of company had arrived. When she didn't get an answer back, she realized that chances were, he was either engaged or out cold. She slipped from the vehicle and into the front seat awkwardly and looked to see if another handgun was in the glove box. And, indeed, there was.

She grabbed it, took a deep breath, and slipped out of the vehicle once more. She crept forward, trying to stay well hidden from everything. And, sure enough, there was Charles and Garret, with guns pointed at them. No sign of Kano, but two men were down on the ground, either dead or unconscious, and three others were busy talking. One gunman reached out and smacked Garret hard in the face. Another poked at Charles, calling him an old man.

"You really thought you would pull one over on us, old man?"

At that, Charles just stood there and smiled.

"Look at that smile on him," the other guy said. "Almost like he has some sort of secret weapon."

"Outside of the girl, nobody was with him, when I saw them."

"And are you sure it was a girl?"

"Yeah," he said, "I am."

"Well, she could be around here somewhere too."

"Better go check the vehicle," he said. "Make sure you take her out. Just a simple pop in the head. No theatrics. Just get the job done."

The one guy took off at a fast pace toward her car. She

stared, wondering what she was supposed to do. She knew that this guy couldn't be allowed to carry on because, in that case, he would come back and tell them she wasn't there. She turned, lined up her shot, and, as he bent down to check inside the back seat of the car, she fired one shot at him. And down he went. She spun back around to the other men to see the two guys laughing.

Garret looked sick.

One of the gunmen said, "Oh, you cared about that one, did you?" He shook his head. "Too damn bad, she's gone now," he said, chuckling. "She wasn't any good anyway. You know that."

Nothing in Garret's face gave away his emotions, except for the clenching of his fists. She could see that easily. She wondered what to do with her next advantage because, if anybody came looking for the guy she'd shot, it would be all over again. She had to make the most of the few moments that she actually had available.

One of the men said, "Let's move these two into the vehicle," he said. "Anybody could come along, and we don't have time for this."

"I suggest we just pop 'em right here," the other said, and he lifted the gun to shoot Charles first. She didn't even think about it and raised her gun and fired once more. The gunman dropped dead.

Garret wasn't sure what the hell was going on, but somebody was on his side, and he was never one to look a gift horse in the mouth. He was on the second gunman before the guy had a chance to even register that his partner was dead. By the time he had the man subdued, he turned and Charles was at his side, but there was no sign of Kano. Then, hearing footsteps, he suddenly looked up to see Kano, standing there with Astra.

She stared at Garret in shock, still holding the handgun. Charles looked at her, smiled, and said, "I see that, like your sister, you can't follow orders."

"And I think this time," she said, "it was the right thing to do. He came to kill me," she murmured.

"And what did you do?" Garret asked softly.

"I was actually already over here, but I realized that, once he found me missing, it would be all over."

"So you shot him?"

"I did. I just don't know if he's dead or not."

With that, Kano took off to check. She walked slowly forward. "I've never killed a man before," she said, feeling her face turning gray.

Garret walked over, wrapped his arms around her, and held her close. "I, for one, am very thankful that you did," he said. "We were goners."

She nodded. "He would have shot Charles," she said, turning to look at Charles. "Why would he do that?"

"Because that's where the maximum pain would be for Garret. They work it out so they take out the weakest ones and make everybody suffer that much longer," Charles murmured.

"Assholes," she said, with feeling.

"It's part of the game."

"There's no game to this," she said. "It's deadly serious."

"That it is," Charles said.

Kano came back, and the look on his face made her swallow. Garret reached up, hugged her close, and said, "Good," he said. "The other guy's dead."

"I didn't think I shot him that badly," she said.

"Maybe not," Kano said, "but you hit an artery, and he

bled out."

She took a slow deep breath. "So do I go to jail now?"

Her voice was so small and tinny that Garret realized she really had no idea. He wrapped her up even closer and said, "No, absolutely not."

"I killed two men," she said, staring at him, her eyes like huge orbs in the darkness.

"You did it to save our lives." At that, Charles was already on the phone. Garret nodded toward Charles and said, "Charles's taking care of it."

"Taking care of what?" she said.

"There won't be any mention of this anywhere," he said. "It'll all go quietly away. I highly doubt these were any exemplary citizens for anybody to be concerned about," he said. "So you'll be fine."

CHAPTER 11

THEY AND JONAS were at Charles's place, and Charles was busy pacing, as Jonas reamed him out. It was all she could do to stand here and to listen. And, when Jonas finally came to a stop, Charles turned and looked at Jonas and then spoke in a calm voice.

"Are you quite finished, young man?" Jonas just glared at him and then sagged in place and nodded. "Good," Charles said. "That, sir, is your free one. See that you never speak to me like that again ..."

Jonas opened his mouth, took one look at Charles, and slammed his mouth shut, then nodded. "Fine," Jonas said, "but this is a shitstorm."

"Yes, it is, but it's not of our making," Garret reminded him. "And we did hand you two live ones."

"It's never your fault," he roared at Garret. "You guys just walk into my country, and all this shit happens. And those two guys know nothing. They will get minor charges but have no clue what's going on."

"You might want to remember that we walked into the country because you guys hadn't found a missing person," Garret snapped right back.

"And now we have two missing people again? The sister, right?" He turned and looked at her. Astra nodded and chose to stay silent. "This is just too unbelievable. I thought you guys were good at this."

"We weren't taking into account the fact that the sister, Amy, might actually listen to somebody in her world to get out of here. She was safe here, if she would have just stayed put."

"Right," Jonas said. "As if that'll happen."

Astra had to admit that she was surprised at Amy's behavior too. "I don't think she thought this would be the outcome."

"Of course not," Jonas said. "I guess we're back to the fact that she's probably not thinking clearly, right?"

"I really hate the fact that everything comes back to blaming it on her pregnancy," she announced. "I get that my sister is doing things in her own way, but she's still in trouble right now, and we need to help her."

"The bottom line is," Jonas said, "we need to get Garret's brother back. That she's now gone missing is just another power play."

"So what will we do to get her back then?"

"I'm not sure," Jonas snapped. "You got any suggestions? It's your sister, after all."

"Ouch," she said, "because the answer is no. I have no clue."

"Neither do I," Jonas said, still clearly frustrated.

"I do," Garret said. "The guy that picked her up is Rick Santino, who used to work for Kingdom Securities. He also offered Gregg a job off the books, private, and Gregg turned him down, according to what we got from Astra, regarding some garbled message from Amy."

"But we don't know how factual any of that is," Astra said.

"We never do." Jonas raised both hands in frustration.

"This is all just hearsay."

"Sure, it is," Garret said, "but it's all we've got."

"Of course it is," Charles grumbled. "I've already got a run happening on this Rick."

"No known residence in town. He's actually a citizen of France," Garret said.

Kano entered the conversation. "So what are the chances that Amy's been taken across the channel?"

"God help us then," Jonas said. "We've got alerts set up, and they are spot-checking everybody going across."

"And would they leave, without my brother?" Garret asked.

"Not yet," Charles said. "I don't think that's the plan. I don't think they want to take these people back to Paris. Absolutely no reason for it."

"No, that's true," Jonas said, "at least no reason we know of."

"And what about Deedee from Kingdom? She said she'd help anyway, right?" Garret asked.

"Yeah, she's playing games," Kano said. "I'll have to go over there and have a personal talk with her."

"Well, you're not going now," Jonas said. "Nobody else is leaving. You're not splitting up. I don't want to track any more of you down again."

"Right," Kano said, looking at Garret. "I've tried to contact her, but she's not being cooperative."

"Gee, what a surprise," he said. "Do you know this Rick guy?"

"No. I really don't," Kano replied.

"But she does?"

"Maybe," he said. "I'm just not sure."

"We need more. We've got to have something more

from her," Garret said.

Kano groaned and pulled out his phone. Moments later, he said, "Deedee, it's Kano."

Everybody else heard the woman laughing loudly on the other end.

"Listen. This Rick? What kind of an asshole is he?"

They couldn't hear the other side of the conversation, so waited, not even pretending not to eavesdrop.

"Great, so one of the worst. And you don't have anything to do with him anymore? You're sure? Okay. You just haven't been very forthcoming with any kind of information, and I know you must have some. I know you want something in return, but right now we've got a problem, since Rick has taken Gregg's girlfriend."

He listened again and nodded. "Yeah, you say you don't know anything about him. But you must know if he has any haunts in England, any places where he'd go? ... He better not. Use your network." Kano sighed loudly. "Well, I don't want him using my network either," he said, "but that doesn't change anything. We still need to have some idea of what he's got going on. We haven't tracked down any of his family, though hopefully he hasn't brought them into this bullshit anyway."

Kano rolled his eyes at his audience. "Good. Okay, let's see what—what do you mean, he has a friend?" Kano shook his head. "You know he's doing deals himself, right?" With that, there was a shout on the other end of the phone. He nodded slowly. "Well, apparently he offered Gregg a private job. What do you know about that?" He grinned. "Well, sorry if that shit's going on right under your nose, but it sounds like it is, and I would think you'd want to do something about it."

Astra listened to the conversation between Kano and this other woman, who was apparently pretty high up in the Kingdom Securities hierarchy. As in possibly the owner now, after taking control a decade ago. Astra was slowly piecing together bits and pieces of what she'd learned. Not only was the airplane explosion supposedly targeted at Bullard, but it had also taken out Garret and another man. Bullard was the only one missing. He had had a relationship with this woman, so the team was looking fairly closely at Kingdom.

Astra quietly asked, "Wouldn't it kind of muck up the business for everyone if one company attacked another?"

Garret looked at her, nodded, and said, "Yeah, but that doesn't mean it's not happening though."

"Do you suspect her?"

He shook his head. "No, I don't think so. She once had a thing for Bullard. Then she always hunted for younger men."

"There's nothing more dead than a dead relationship," she said.

He smiled. "I get that," he said, "but, in this case, I think she really did care for him."

Astra nodded and didn't say anything for a moment. "She doesn't seem to know what's going on in her own backyard though."

"And that seemed to be a bit of a surprise to her," he said. "That's interesting because that means she doesn't have her fingers on all the pulses that she thought she did."

"Which is bad news for everybody," she murmured.

Finally Kano got off the phone. He looked at them and said, "There is a friend here in town who apparently this Rick guy spent a lot of time with. Deedee did not know anything about private jobs, and she's fairly unimpressed with the concept," he said, "so that's one thing."

"But it's not enough," Garret said, "not enough for anything yet."

"No, you're right," Kano said. "We still have to do some more digging."

"Not just more digging," he said. "The issue is, we've got to find these people, and we've got to find them now."

"And what about the threat I got?" Astra asked, worried about her sister.

"Yeah," he said, "I'm still trying to figure out if that's a diversion or not. Obviously your sister's been taken."

"What is it they want with your brother?"

"I don't know. It doesn't sound like they necessarily have my brother either," he said. "That threat was fairly ambiguous. Just *we've got your sister.*"

"I know," she said, "and they want your brother."

"Which means they don't have him. So we've got two parties going here, one that's got him and one that doesn't but wants him."

"What about the guy at the bar who was looking after him, who wanted Gregg moved?"

"The dead gopher guy? We got an ID on him. Running that," Garret said.

"At the first bar, right? So, instead of searching Maggie's place, which place do we need to go back and check on?"

At that, Charles popped up. "Maggie's home is under surveillance, and there's been no activity at her place, at all."

"Dammit," Garret said. "I was hoping they would still go there, but, of course, as soon as there was a problem, that place became off-limits."

"Still, the gopher guy had to be holding Gregg somewhere," she murmured. "We should find that."

"We're tracking his vehicle location," Garret said. "So far we haven't found any place that he would have taken Gregg that was his own property."

"And now we've expanded on the places that the bar owner owns."

"I guess it could be anybody, couldn't it?" Astra asked.

"Absolutely," Garret said, "and chances are, it is anybody. It's just never as clear-cut as we want it to be."

"And that's just ridiculous." She got up and paced. "We need this to come to a conclusion."

"Yes," Charles said gently, "but, if we rush things, we'll get people killed."

She raised her hands in frustration and flung herself onto the couch. "So you've got people running down all these leads, right?"

Charles, Garret, and Kano all nodded. Even Jonas. On that point, they all agreed.

"And, so far, nothing?"

"Correct."

"So why don't we go back to good old-fashioned threats," she said. "Go back to the pub owner and pound him into the ground. Wouldn't that be simpler?"

"I like it," Garret said, with a big smile. "But?"

"I feel like I'm missing something," she said.

Jonas nodded.

"You are," Garret said. "We've already got information on that guy's house—the first bar owner—and we're checking to see if there's any chance Gregg is there."

"You don't want to just go threaten him?"

"Well, he won't be alone. It's hardly legal, and what we don't want to do is get caught or push any panic buttons, so that he moves Gregg, and we can never find him."

"But wouldn't it be easier to find Gregg in transit, instead of squirreled away somewhere?"

"Only if we knew where he was. That's what we were hoping to do earlier. We wanted to grab Gregg, while he was being moved this last time. Only he wasn't there."

She sat back, closed her eyes, and whispered, "This is so wrong."

"You deal with this all the time in your job, don't you?" Charles asked.

Jonas listened with interest.

"Not really," she said. "Other people deal with this kind of frustration level. It's not really something that touches my aspect of the job. I know what we're always working on, and I get involved, and we get big cases, but I'm not the one sitting there at the computer, working my way through all these processes."

"Oh, so this gives you a whole new understanding, doesn't it?" Charles asked.

"And a whole new level of frustration, yes," she said, with a smile. "And that'll be an issue."

"Okay, so then what?" Garret asked.

"I don't know," she said.

Kano, looking up from his laptop, suddenly said, "I do. This Rick guy, who's holding Amy and wants Gregg, Rick doesn't have a full brother, but he has a half brother. And the half brother lives in town."

"In town, in town?" Astra asked.

"No, not in town, just outside of town, at an old farmhouse," Kano explained.

"That sounds positive. That's certainly an interesting location. How often has anybody been there?" Garret asked.

"Seems brother actually lives there, so there should be a

fair bit of traffic," Kano said.

"I'm coming this time too," she said.

Garret and Kano stopped and glared at her. She shrugged. "For all you know, my sister's there," she said. "And, if that's the case, you won't want to deal with her."

The men looked at each other but back at her and frowned.

Charles chuckled. "She's right, you know? If Amy is there, which is quite possible, then you'll need somebody to look after her."

"Speaking of which," Kano said, "did we get any intel on the vehicle she got into?"

"We only had the basic model," Charles said, "and it disappeared into a parking lot and never came out."

"Is anybody looking to see who's in the parking lot?" Garret asked, looking straight at Jonas.

"Yeah, we found it deserted and checked it already," Jonas said. "It's empty."

"So they moved her into another vehicle then?"

"Yes," Jonas said. "And, yes, I know. We have traffic cams all around there. We're tracking that, but over three hundred vehicles came and went."

"During that hour?"

"No, not during that hour," he said, "but what I can tell you is that not one vehicle went out with two people sitting upright."

"So she was either stashed in the trunk or lying down in the back seat?"

Jonas nodded. "And, yes, of course we're tracking all of those, but that's a lot of vehicles and a lot of data to sort through."

"Right, and we don't have any connection to Rick."

Kano held up his phone. "I just got an address for him, and it looks like they're only maybe two miles apart."

"Do you think they're connected?"

"I wouldn't think so, but who knows?" he said.

The men just looked at each other and then turned and stared at her.

"I don't care what you say," she said. "I need to come."

"It's safer if you stay here," Garret said.

"As long as I stay inside, you mean?"

"Absolutely, and Charles's staying this time, so he can run command central from here."

"I'm not staying," she said smoothly. "I'm coming with you."

"Why?" Garret asked, sincerely curious.

"I already told you, about my sister," she said. "And there's another aspect, which is that this is the part of the job that I never see, and I think I'll be a better person and better at my job if I do see this part."

"You better be careful what you wish for," Garret said. "A lot of ugliness is out there."

She stood up straight, shoved her hands into her pockets, and glared at him. "I already killed two men tonight," she said. "At some point in time, after all this, I'll have to deal with that. But, right now, I'm dealing with the loss of my sister. Through her own foolishness, she's got herself caught up in something very ugly again. Let's just get her out of this, please, and find your brother."

He took a slow deep breath, looked at her and then Kano, who shrugged.

"Let's go," Kano said. "We're wasting time."

GARRET DIDN'T KNOW how he felt about bringing Astra again. She was here, and she was safe at the moment, but she was right. If Amy were there, it could get difficult. At the same time, he didn't really want Astra to see any more of the ugliness of the seedier side of life. As they grabbed up jackets, he warned her, "You may not like what you see."

"I never like what I see in my job," she said, with all seriousness.

He thought about the work she did and nodded. "At least there's a sense of satisfaction at the end of the day."

"Only on the good days," she said. "Some of these cases take years."

"I know," he said. "Some of ours do too. They're just—" And he stopped. He wrapped an arm around her shoulder and led her through to the other apartment. "We're going out a different way," he said. "Nobody uses the front door."

"Is that why it's got the alarm set?"

"Charles sets the alarms anytime he's inside or when he leaves," he said. "He's been caught off guard once too many times for peace of mind."

"It's also very difficult," she murmured. "He takes it so easily."

"He's very good at what he does, and he's been doing this for a very long time."

"I can imagine," she said. "It's still a surprise though."

"Of course it is. You don't expect anybody in his generation to be active in this. But you know? He's been doing it for so long, I'm not sure he could stop."

"He should be sitting in front of a fireplace, with a partner," she said. "Having tea and cookies."

"Don't write him off. He's not that old," Garret warned. "He'd be insulted if you thought he was past his prime."

She chuckled. "There's nothing *past prime* about him," she said. "He's heading into a wonderful age group, and he's so very graceful."

"He also has some of the best self-defense moves you've ever seen," he said. "Like I said, don't think you know him. There's a reason he does the work he does."

She nodded slowly. "So easy to place people into little boxes that fit what we think they are, isn't it?"

"That's one of the biggest lessons about the work we do," Kano said. "Learning not to pigeonhole people but to open up your mind and see what people really are like. Whether it's what you want to see them as or not. And that's kind of hard too because, seeing those people, and what they can do to others, it's just disgusting."

"It is," Garret said. "That's another reason why it's so important that we take as many of these guys off the streets as we can."

"We don't get many of them off though, do we?" she asked, as he led her downstairs and into the vehicle. "It seems like all we end up with is more slime."

"I'd like to think we're winning the war," he said. "Technology's made that both easier and harder because a lot of the scumbags out there are techies as well."

"Yeah," she said. "That's where we come in."

"So you know exactly what I'm talking about." He helped her into the back of the vehicle and said, "Now let's go."

She sighed, buckled up, and said, "Don't write me off either. I might not have the skills that you guys have, but I have a lot of common sense."

"Glad you got that, but not your sister," he said, "because I don't know what she's thinking."

"I suspect she saw Rick as a friend, somebody she could go out with and spend a few hours in a pub," she said quietly. "Of course that's the opposite of what he is, but Amy wouldn't have seen an enemy coming. She's just not the kind of person to see it."

"Is she stupid?" Kano asked.

"Not stupid, per se, but naive," Astra said, "definitely naive." She was seated in the back, with both Garret and Kano in the front, Kano driving, while Garret brought up the addresses they were heading to. Jonas remained at Charles's house, tidying things up about the murders. The car ride to the potential country residences, where Gregg could be held, was silent for twenty minutes, until they came close to the first house in question. Lights were on, and several vehicles were parked in front. Loud laughter came from inside.

She leaned forward and said, "That doesn't look likely."

"Why is that?" Garret asked, interested to hear her response.

"Well, surely it wouldn't be party time, if something like a kidnapping was going on, would it?"

"Well, it's a great way to hide what's going on in the deep dark recesses of a house. Nobody would hear him screaming."

"Oh, God," she said and sank back.

He wasn't sorry he'd said that because absolutely nothing was clean, neat, or tidy about this business. It was quite possible to stage such a gathering, if somebody wanted something from Gregg and if he were being tortured in an attempt to get it. Garret looked at Kano. "I suggest you leave me here, and you and Astra go drive past the other address and check that out."

"Yeah, that's what I was thinking," he said. "You okay alone?"

"No, he's not," she said.

"I'm okay," Garret replied, and, without giving her a chance to say anything, he slipped from the vehicle and morphed into the shadows.

GARRET LIVED IN the shadows, and it seemed he loved the shadows in a way. It's where he was comfortable, and an awful lot could be accomplished there, as long as he had a bit of room to work. He knew she didn't like it one bit, but that was just too bad. It was one of the things that she must get used to, if or when they ever decided to see each other on a less formal basis. Certainly that relationship was something he wanted to pursue, but he wasn't so sure about her. He kept catching something in her gaze every once in a while, and he wasn't sure what that was all about.

He knew Charles had made a point earlier and then had nodded at him a couple times, as if to say, "Come on, boy. Step up." But Garret wasn't sure what was supposed to happen with that either. His wasn't an easy business to be in and to also have a relationship. He'd tried it with Amy and had to admit that it had been a really shitty decision on his part. He couldn't blame her for that, but, at the same time, it wasn't exactly a decision made with much intelligence.

That was sad too, because Amy had deserved more than he'd given. Apparently she needed a lot more, and he just hadn't known. It still burned him to think of what she and his brother did, but it no longer bothered him with the same intensity. He could now clearly see Amy as completely unsuited for him and realized that, as much as he didn't want her, he probably should thank his brother for taking her off his hands.

As he walked to the house, he saw a woman in the kitchen. She answered a phone call, put it down, and then proceeded to fill a tray with food. He wondered if she was taking that to a prisoner, in which case, that would make for an awesome opportunity for Garret. He followed her movements, as she picked up the tray and headed out to the room up above the garage. But, as soon as a man let her in, she put down the tray, turned around, and threw her arms around him. It was obvious that her visit had been for something completely different than checking up on a prisoner. Unless his brother was the prisoner. As he studied the man's frame, which was taller and skinnier than his brother, Garret knew he was going in the wrong direction there.

He made his way back to the kitchen, stepped inside, and listened to the conversation in the other room, but the men were involved in a poker game, accompanied by their raucous laughter, were also talking about some play in the latest football game. They were arguing, but it was good-natured, as if this group of guys came together on a regular basis to play cards or to watch sports.

Finding the basement door, Garret quickly stepped downstairs and searched. When he found nothing there, he texted Kano and said, "This looks clean. Come pick me up."

"I'm already on my way back. Be there in five."

Garret made his way up and realized somebody was in the kitchen. He just strode across the room, as if he were meant to be here, and headed out to the porch.

He heard somebody yell behind him, "Hey, what are you doing?" So Garret turned and quickly booked it over the fence. At that, he heard more calls behind him. "Somebody was just in your house," the man roared.

Men threw back chairs, and Garret heard the ruckus, but he was over one fence, over a second fence, and now heading for the copse of trees on the side. He knew the men would be after him as fast as they could get here, but Garret was counting on the fact that Kano was coming to pick him up. Sure enough, by the time the vehicle got there, he was on the other side of the trees, still hiding in the darkness. He dashed out, making Kano hit the brakes, while Garret hopped into the front seat, and they took off, fast. Men came out through the trees behind them, but all they could see, at that point in time, were the taillights. He turned to look at Astra, checking in on her.

She stared at him. "That was a little close," she said quietly.

"It was," he said, "but we're good."

"You're sure?" she said.

"Yeah," he said, then faced Kano. "Somebody is in the room over the garage, but it doesn't appear to be a prisoner. If that were my brother, no way he would have been imprisoned and yet free to walk around like that. He'd be out the window and on his way to freedom."

"From what I know of Gregg, that is quite true," she said.

Turning to her again, he grinned. "It's all good."

She just shook her head and sank back.

He faced Kano. "What did you find?"

"A definite possibility," he said. "We'll be there in a few minutes, and you can give me your take."

As they pulled up to another property, Garret noted the house was set farther back, making it much harder to see anything. A single light was on outside the front door, and a single vehicle was parked in front; that was it. "Interesting."

"This is his brother's house," Kano said. "I've checked the property records. It's been in his family for generations, but the property tax payments are in arrears for at least the last two years."

"So it could be something, could be nothing."

"Exactly."

Garret hopped out and said, "I'll be right back."

CHAPTER 12

"DON'T YOU THINK you should go with him this time?" Astra asked Kano anxiously.

"No, he's just doing reconnaissance. If it looks more promising than anything we've seen so far," he said, "then I'll go help him."

"I hear you," she said, "but I just think he takes a lot of chances. One of these days, those chances will be too much."

"That goes for all of us," he said. "It goes for anybody driving, for that matter. One day your number's up. No way to know when, how, or how far away that day is."

"I know," she said. "Even in my business, we always talk about getting in a hurry and making a mistake one day. We remind ourselves that, if we stick with it, we'll catch them."

"Exactly, and one day you will. Everybody that's on your docket, everybody that's on your radar, one day you'll get them."

"I think patience is the hardest thing to learn," she murmured.

"Many people don't ever learn it," Kano said. "Something like this, there's no easy way out, and there's no easy way forward," he murmured. "All we can do is wait."

"God, it seems like all I've done so far is wait."

Just then the car door opened, and she faced a handgun. She stared at it in shock. "Ah, Kano?" but he'd been knocked out in the front seat. "Shit," she said. She looked at the stranger, grinning at her. "Who the hell are you?"

"Your sister's looking for you," he said.

She stared at him in shock. "Have you got my sister?"

"I do," he said. "Come on. Let's go. I'll put the two of you together." As he dragged her from the car, she tried to look back at Kano. "What did you do to him?"

"Nothing compared to what we'll do to Gregg," he said. "You shouldn't have come here."

"I didn't want to come," she said, desperately searching for answers that would get this guy to understand why she was there. "We're looking for my sister though. She said that Rick had her." She studied the goon. "I don't think you're Rick though."

"No, I'm not," he said. "Rick is my brother."

"Right, that was the only connection we had."

"Of course," he said. "My stupid brother just couldn't keep me out of it."

"Well, there weren't a whole lot of choices in this instance," she said. "Do you have my sister?"

He rolled his eyes. "Didn't I just say that?"

"Maybe," she said. "I'm desperate to find her." Rick's brother shoved her toward the house, and Astra could only hope that Garret saw her.

Her gunman asked, "What were you guys doing here?"

"I wanted a chance to see the house, to see if I should call the police," she said matter-of-factly.

"Well, that ain't going to work," he said.

"Apparently not," she said. "I still don't understand what you want with her."

"It's actually her boyfriend we want."

"Well, he's missing," she said, giving him a hard look.

"Are you telling me that you don't have him?"

"No, we don't, but that's the end game."

"I still don't understand why. Why does anybody want him?"

"Hard to say," he said. "It's all about information."

"So you just won't tell me?"

"Why should I?" he said easily. "For all I know, you're wired."

"Wired?"

Just enough puzzlement was in her tone that he groaned. "You and your sister are two of a kind."

"Somehow that doesn't seem very complimentary," she snapped.

He chuckled. "No, it sure as hell isn't. Nothing but dumb broads, ... both of you."

Inside, she was elated because, as long as he thought that of her in that way, he wouldn't put too much stock into anything that she might do. And, as she'd already learned, there wasn't a whole lot she wouldn't do to protect those she cared about.

As they walked closer to the residence, she said, "Wow, this is a gorgeous house."

He jerked her arm, hard, and said, "It is, and it takes an awful lot of upkeep to keep it that way," he said. "It's been in the family for generations, so I won't let it go now."

"Ah," she said. "You need money."

"Doesn't everybody?" he snarled. "And you're worth money."

"Wrong. No, I'm not," she said. "I don't know who told you that, but I'm really not."

"Oh, I think you are," he said. "I just have to find out who'll pay."

"Well, I'm the only one who would have paid for my sister, and there's nobody else to pay for either of us, if you've got us both," she said in a reasonable tone.

He didn't even comment on that.

"Besides, it's not money for us you want anyway, right? It's actually her fiancé, isn't it?"

"Are they actually engaged? God, he is welcome to her. All she does is complain."

Astra hid her smile at his comment because that was such a perfect description of her sister. "That doesn't mean she's not terrified," she said.

"Oh, she's terrified all right. All she wants is him."

"Well, of course she does. She loves him, and she's been worried sick about him."

"Well, he can have her, if we can find him ourselves."

"And that's where the trouble lies. So you weren't the ones who kidnapped him?"

"Yeah, we were, and we stashed him with somebody, only that somebody moved him."

Her eyes widened at that. "Ouch," she said. "Betrayed from within. That sucks."

"In a big way," he said. "Now would you just stop talking."

She was silent for a few moments, until they entered the big house.

He twisted her arm and said, "Wait here." And he let her go. She stood here, rubbing her sore wrists and easing the pain in her shoulders. She looked around; the house had very little in the way of lights on. She didn't know if that was because of the cost of the power or if it was part of the ambient mood he was trying to maintain. She turned and realized he hadn't left; he'd just been standing behind her, looking for something. Something he then looped around her hands.

She looked at it in dismay. "Is that really necessary?"

"Don't want you to do anything to get away," he said. "One sister's bad enough to look after. I'm not chasing around after the two of you."

He dragged her forward into the kitchen, where her sister sat at the kitchen table with a cup of tea. Astra stared at her sister and asked, "Amy, are you okay?"

Amy hopped up, only her hands were tied too, and so were her feet. She looked up at her sister and started to cry.

"Oh, Amy," Astra said. She walked over to her sister and, even though her hands were tied with a rope hanging off of them, she lifted them over her sister's neck and just held her close.

"I trusted Rick," Amy said.

"Remember that thing about trust?"

"No, you're the one who never trusts anybody," Amy said. "I've always trusted everyone." She wiggled out of Astra's hold and sat down again.

Astra didn't say anything to that because it was true. It's just that she'd always wished her sister wouldn't trust everyone so easily. She sat down beside her sister and asked again, "Are you okay?"

Amy nodded and looked at her guard. "Not that he cares," she snarled.

Astra was surprised to see that kind of spirit in her sister in this situation, but it was a good sign. She looked at her captor. "Any chance I could have a cup of tea too?"

He groaned, as he rolled his eyes at her. "What the hell do you guys think this is? Some kind of Taj Mahal?"

"I guess tea's expensive," Astra said apologetically.

He glared at her. "I'm not that broke." With that, he turned and put the teakettle on the stove.

She watched every move he made. At the same time, Amy stared at Astra, hope in her eyes. Astra looked at her and asked, "What did Rick say to you?"

"Just that I had a bigger purpose."

"Yeah, they're trying to find Gregg," she said.

"Find Gregg?"

Astra nodded. "Apparently they lost him," she said, adding a certain emphasis to the word *lost*.

At that, Amy's eyes widened. "Oh, my God. Oh, my God, did they hurt him?"

"I'm not sure they've hurt him at all," she said. "It's just that he's disappeared. They had somebody looking after him, but either that person betrayed them or something happened to him. The bottom line is that they can't find Gregg now."

"Maybe he got free," she cried out joyfully.

"In which case, that's bad news for you," her captor said. "It's not like I need you guys, if we can't get him anyway."

"Isn't that the leverage you'll use?" Astra asked him. "Telling Gregg that you've got his girlfriend and her sister, so he would come and trade himself for us?"

"You don't know Gregg all that well if you think that'll work," he sneered. "That's not the kind of guy he is."

Her sister glared at him. "He is so. He is very honorable."

The guy laughed. "God, where does she get this shit from?" he said. "Gregg's nothing more than a mark, and he works for a company that's an even bigger mark, and that's it. The guy is full of all kinds of shit. The fact that he's actually got you suckered into it just means you're an easy lay."

At that, her sister started bawling.

He turned around and said to Astra, "Get her to shut the fuck up."

Astra immediately pulled Amy into her arms and whispered, "You need to be quiet."

Amy's sobs dampened down slightly. "I'm so sorry," she said. "You told me to stay put, and I didn't listen."

"Yes, I did," Astra said in a wry tone. "But you never were very good at following instructions."

Her sister sniffled and said, "I'm getting better."

She didn't say anything to that, since she hadn't seen any sign of it. "I get that you just wanted out for a bit."

"I wanted Gregg," she said. "I thought for sure Rick could help. They work together. Gregg knows him. Rick knows the guys they worked with in the past. That's got to be what this is all about," she said. "It has to be somebody else from an old case that's after him."

"Maybe," Astra said, "but I wouldn't count on it."

At that, their gunman turned and looked at her and asked, "What do you know?"

"I don't know jack shit," Astra said, with a smirk. "All I know is that he's missing. I don't know anything about the work he does. I barely even know this Rick guy," she said. "Who is he?"

"None of your business," he snapped.

She nodded and just stayed close to her sister. But he did deliver a cup of tea, strong, black, with no milk or sugar. Astra politely said, "Thank you."

He nodded, grabbed the loose end of her rope, and tied it to her sister's chair. "Now you're not fucking going anywhere," he said.

Astra just sat here, crestfallen, looking beaten down and

upset, so he would think that she actually was. The last thing she wanted him to realize was that Kano wasn't the only one who had been with her in the car, and she didn't want anybody to go back outside and finish the job on him. All she had to do now was keep her and her sister both alive and wait for the cavalry or for their own opening to escape.

GARRET CHECKED FOR a pulse on Kano's wrist. He was down as low as he could be to the ground, right next to the vehicle, his gaze constantly scanning the area around him. Even as he checked, he could feel something surging through him, and then he realized it was Kano's pulse.

Kano groaned.

"Take it easy," Garret said. "You've been hit over the head."

"Where am I?" Kano said, reaching up to rub his forehead.

"You're still in the car," he said, "but I don't think it'll be long before somebody comes back to check on you." He quickly opened the vehicle, helped Kano out, and moved him into the trees. Once in the shadows, he sat him back down on the ground. "Astra's been taken."

Kano stared at him in shock.

"I'm not sure how he got the jump on you," Garret said.

"I don't know. He came out of nowhere. I'd just turned to say something to her and got clobbered on the head. I don't remember anything after that."

"Well, I saw her being led into the house, and I heard part of the conversation. They have Amy too."

"Well, that's a good thing," he said. "We've got two of them now."

"Exactly. And, at the same time, they're still looking for Gregg. Apparently the guy trying to convince the boss to let Gregg go had moved him. He might have known more about what was going on and what they would do with him. Anyway, he moved Gregg, and these guys—who kidnapped Gregg in the first place—can't find him now."

"Shit," Kano said. "That's not good, … for a couple reasons. Gregg could be someplace where time is running out on him."

"And it's possible that we won't ever find out where he is."

"We have to track that asshole's movements," Kano said.

"Oh, I hear you," he said. "I'm doing what I can, but, right now, we have to get the girls. I've already told Charles, and he's on it. They're tracking the dead courier's life to find out where he could have moved Gregg. Chances are it'll be not too far away. But we have to get there before anything else happens to Gregg."

"I wonder why the courier backtracked, protecting Gregg?"

"Something Gregg said maybe."

"It's possible. Who the hell knows?" Kano stood up experimentally and gave his head a shake. "Damn, that'll be a bit of a bitch for a while."

"That's okay. You're up. You're moving. You're alive," Garret said. "We've got to remember that."

"Yeah, and I owe that asshole for the headache," he said. He turned to face the house. "How many in there?"

"That's the problem," he said. "I only saw one, and that makes no sense to me."

"He's the guard on duty? Maybe he's the one waiting for the others to come back."

"Most likely," Garret said, "so we don't have much time."

"No, we don't have any time," he said.

"So let's go, if you're up to it."

Kano shot him a hard look. "Oh, I'm up to it," he said. Blood still trickled down the side of his head, but he ignored it and said, "Let's go."

CHAPTER 13

SEATED IN THE kitchen, Astra watched the gunman's movements. He kept looking out the window constantly, as if waiting for somebody else.

She whispered to Amy, "Is anybody else here?"

Amy looked at her and looked at him, but he appeared not to have heard. She held up three fingers and then shrugged.

So three people were here, or at least Amy had seen three, but where were the other two? Were they still around here or had they left the property, out looking for Gregg?

It was a case of so many questions and no answers again.

"I still don't understand why you want Gregg," Astra stated, facing the gunman.

"You don't have to understand," he said. "I told you to shut the fuck up. Do I need to tell you again? Because I'll tell you with my fists the next time."

She shut up for a while, looking at Amy.

Amy nodded and turned her head a bit, so Astra could see the side of her face, which was puffy.

Her glare deepened. "You actually hit a tied-up woman?" she said. "What kind of an asshole are you?"

"An asshole who doesn't have a problem hitting her nosy sister either," he said. "I've got things to do and places to be, and I really don't need to be here, listening to you."

"Ahh," she said. "So you're waiting for somebody now, aren't you?"

"Yeah, I am," he said. "And they ain't coming any faster with your noise rattling around."

"Sorry," she said cheerfully.

He just glared at her.

"You know that, if you put us in a bedroom and let us lie down, we wouldn't be bothering you," she said.

He looked like he would almost consider it; then he shook his head. "No way," he said. "I'm keeping you right where I can see you."

"Okay," she said agreeably. He looked at her suspiciously, but she just sipped her tea. She was totally okay to be here too, because it meant that the men would find them easily. As she sat here, Amy looked at her.

"I don't know what happened to Gregg," she said tearfully.

"Just have some faith," she said, "that this will all work out."

The guy sneered. "Oh, yeah, it'll all work out." And then he gave a big laugh. "Such a loser."

Amy's face twisted again.

Astra held up her hand and said, "Don't bother, Amy. It'll be fine. Don't cry."

Taking several long deep breaths, Amy searched her sister's face.

Astra tried to give her a reassuring smile, but it was a little hard, considering the asshole remained in the room with them. Astra nodded toward the front door.

Amy frowned at her, looked toward the front door, and back. She raised one eyebrow and then gave a clipped nod. Immediately Amy sank back and stared.

Astra shrugged, sipped her tea, and motioned at Amy's tea. "Drink up the tea," she said. "It will make you feel better." Amy sipped it quietly, as Astra studied the gunman.

He walked from window to window and back again, obviously struggling with impatience. And frankly, as long as he was impatient, that was good news for them. Now all Astra needed was for the good guys to come. She could only hope that Kano was okay and that he was there to help bolster whatever move Garret decided to make. Charles was right; she had to trust in their skills, ability, and judgment to do whatever they needed to do in any given situation. Regardless of how that might look to anybody else.

So many things in life were important that nobody really understood, and this was one of them. It was all about trust. And, for Garret, that was an even bigger issue now. Astra didn't agree with what her sister had done, but, after seeing Amy and Gregg together, witnessing how deep their feelings appeared to run, Astra understood. They could have proceeded with their relationship in a better way, but, at the same time, at least it left an open field for Astra and Garret.

The gunman turned and looked at Astra. "What's that look on your face for?" he snapped.

Immediately she dropped her expression and stared at him steadily. "I was thinking of happier times," she said.

"Yeah, well, keep thinking of them," he said, "because all you'll have is memories."

"And why is that?" she said.

"Because, by the time this is over," he said, "you'll probably be dead."

"No need for that," she said. "I don't know anything, and neither does my sister."

"Says you," he sneered.

"It's obvious you're waiting for somebody to come," she said, "so I don't know why you're getting all pissy at me, when it's them you're mad at."

"Because you are where you don't belong," he snapped.

"I was looking for my sister," she said, with a motion at Amy. Amy stayed quiet and just shuffled a little closer to her. "What else would I be doing?"

"Well, you shouldn't have come," he said, turning to lean against the counter. And, just as he did that, she thought she saw movement behind him.

She nodded slowly. "I get that. So let me and my sister go," she said, "and we'll disappear out of your life completely."

He laughed. "Too late for that, bitch," he said. "You made your choice. Now you'll have to pay for it."

"Surely we can talk about this," Astra said fearfully.

"No," he said. "And you sure as hell can't offer me enough money to backtrack on what I'm doing here. That's not worth my life."

"Killing people who have nothing to do with anything?" she asked.

"Yeah, exactly," he said.

"How did you lose Gregg in the first place?"

"We didn't lose him," he snapped. "I told you that."

"Right. Why did the other guy betray you and let Gregg go then?"

"He didn't let him go," he said. "He moved Gregg. Big difference."

She nodded slowly. "I guess," she said. "Why would he do that?"

"Because he's a double-crossing asshole, I imagine," he said. "I don't know why else he'd do it."

"Unless he had sympathy for Gregg."

"I don't give a shit how much sympathy he had for him. He had a job to do. That's all there is to it."

She nodded slowly. "I guess, but it's kind of sad."

"Not sad at all," he snapped. "It is what it is."

"I just don't understand what it would take to have somebody go against all this, knowing that his life would be in danger."

He scratched his face and said, "Honestly I don't know either. It makes no sense to me."

"Okay," she said. "Hopefully we'll both get some answers."

"Not likely," he sneered. "The only answers you'll get are the ones you don't want to hear."

"Such as?" she challenged.

"Such as what'll happen to you," he said.

"And we're back to that again. I can pay you."

"You just finished telling me that you couldn't pay for your sister."

"Yeah, I can hardly pay to set my sister free, if I'm here. You've taken both of us. I would pay for her, and she would pay for me, but, with both of us here, obviously we can't do either."

He rolled his eyes at her. "You're an idiot."

She stayed quiet, wondering who the hell the idiot in the room really was. But no point in arguing with him. She just smiled and said, "It's not the first time I've been called that."

"Usually that's the term reserved for me," Amy said.

"Not so bad though, was it?" Astra said.

"It was terrible," she said. "You were always the brainy one. You were the one everybody loved. I wanted everyone to love me, but we weren't alike at all."

"No," she said. "And we still aren't. I am much calmer, more reserved, whereas you are a little more naive, and a whole lot more about the fun in life."

"But I have heart," her sister argued.

And, at that, Astra looked at her, smiled, and said, "You do, indeed. We have to remember that, no matter how this all turns out. We have to remember that heart is what's important."

"Spare me the sob story," the guy snapped. "Nobody gives a shit."

Amy just smiled, a little teary-eyed, then reached across and grabbed Astra's hand. "Please tell me that we'll make it through this." Her gaze fell to her belly.

"I'll tell you what. We'll do everything we can together to make it through this," Astra promised her. "We both deserve a happy future."

Amy sat back and sighed. "I just want Gregg," she murmured.

"Got it," she said. "You don't mind if I pick up Garret then, do you?"

Amy looked at her in surprise and then started laughing. "Oh my," she said. "You know what? That makes so much more sense, when I think about it."

"Right, you've no idea how jealous I was way back when."

"You should have said something," Amy said. "Because, oh, my gosh, that would have been so much better for him too."

"Well, you saw him first," she said. "So I kind of had to wait until it was over with."

"Are you two serious? Are you fucking serious? You're sitting here talking about your boyfriends?" Their kidnapper stared at them in shock and disgust.

"Why not?" Astra asked with a smile. "Is that something we can't talk about?"

He stared at her in disbelief. "You know you'll fucking die in the next couple hours, right?"

Amy gripped her fingers really tight.

Astra glared at him. "You don't have to upset my sister like that," she snapped.

He shook his head. "Get a grip," he said. "This isn't a bloody tea party."

She looked at her teacup, smiled, lifted it up, and said, "Actually it is. So here's to us and to whatever the future brings." With that, she had a big sip of tea.

GARRET HAD COME up to the house, was at the back door to the kitchen, while Kano was doing a search around the outside. Garret wasn't sure what he saw. Both Amy and Astra sat close together, almost too close for comfort in normal circumstances, and yet Astra had a smile on her face, and she appeared to be talking to the man at the window. And it was a monster of a man at that.

When Garret felt the buzz of his phone, he pulled it out to see a note from Kano, saying he'd taken one down. With that, Garret swore under his breath. They hadn't seen anybody else here, but it made sense that a guard would be outside somewhere. Garret could only hope just one guy was inside the house. At the moment he didn't know if anybody else was being held prisoner in there, besides Amy and Astra. His brother being here would be too easy. But Garret sure as hell hoped he was.

Just then another vehicle pulled up, and he heard the

engine slowing down. He frowned at that, sent Kano a quick message, and waited, studying the kitchen layout. The big guy straightened, when he heard the noise, and strode to the kitchen window, but he turned and pointed an admonishing finger at the two women. Then he disappeared from sight.

Garret slipped inside immediately, cut their bonds, pulled them out the back door, and whispered, "Head to the trees in the far corner." Both of them took off without any argument, and, for that, he was grateful. He sent Kano another message, as Garret eased farther into the kitchen, closer to the front room.

He looked for anything that could be used as a big weapon to help take down the big man. He had his hand-gun, and that would do to a certain extent, but he'd seen guys with multiple bullet holes in them still plowing forward. He heard the big monster heading down the front porch steps, yelling and snarling at whoever had just arrived.

"About fucking time you got here," he snapped. "What the hell?"

"We're here. We're here," he said. "Shut your hole, and don't get your panties in a twist."

The big guy snorted. "You should be damn lucky if I do because, right now, I want to twist your heads off. You left me with those two little bitches."

"Hey," he said. "That was the easy job."

"Well, did you find the asshole at least?"

"Hell yeah, we got him," he said.

Garret stepped back and shifted, so he could look at the vehicle to see who they were talking about, and, sure enough, his brother was being unloaded from the car by one guy. Garret stared at Gregg and swore under his breath. Gregg wasn't moving on his own power; his face looked like it had taken a beating, and his leg was dragging behind him. Not cool. On top of that, two more men had arrived with him, accompanied with a lot of raucous shouting. So the odds now were four to two.

He really wanted Kano to stay with the women, but he also knew that Kano wouldn't. And neither would the women let him. The problem was, if the women got into the midst of this mess, they would never know who was where.

Luckily the driver got back into the car and took off. Three to two were better odds. Still, he sent a quick message to Kano with an update and asked him to make sure the women stayed in the trees.

After that, Garret slipped into one of the closets alongside the hallway, hoping for a place to hide where he could listen in and see just what the hell was going on here. As soon as he was in position, the front door slammed right beside him, and the guys talked among themselves.

"So this guy had him out in a shed, where he used to work. Damn near took us forever to find him."

"Well, you got him," said the big man from the house. "That should save our butts."

"Maybe," the first guy said, with a little less joviality in his voice.

"She's a hard-ass bitch," said a third man.

"Any idea why they wanted him?"

"No, and I don't give a shit. Our job was to grab him, to keep him, and to move him back to France."

"Not going to be so easy," one guy murmured.

"It never is, but we don't have any other options right now."

"Did you send a message, saying we had him? When do they want him moved?"

"Yeah, we're supposed to hold him here. Apparently she needs to take care of some other interference."

"Maybe, but that doesn't affect us."

"No, but we need to get paid."

"Damn," he said. "I want this over with and this asshole gone, before somebody else tries to spring him loose."

"Yeah, well, just think about it," he said. "We've got the two women, and we got him, so we'll pass them all over, and they can deep-six the whole lot of them. I don't give a shit, as long as it keeps us free and clear."

"Yeah, yeah, yeah," he said. They were sitting in a living room, with Gregg sitting slumped on one end of the couch. Garret studied his brother's face through the crack in the closet door, but it was hard to see how badly hurt he was or whether he was putting it on.

Just like Garret, his brother knew exactly how to play the game. If the bad guys thought you were more injured than you actually were, they eased up security. At least that's what Garret hoped was going on, but it was all too possible that his brother was severely injured as well. And that would just make Garret even angrier.

"Do we know anything?"

"I already told you," he said.

"I just want to get paid," the second man said, in a tone turning whiny.

"We all want to get paid," the huge man said. "It's the only reason we're doing this."

"Yeah, did you ever think about that? You know? Whether or not there's some guy up at them pearly gates, looking down at us, and saying, *Hell no, you're not coming in here. Look at what you did in your life.*"

"No," the big man said. "I sure as hell don't think about

that at all."

"Don't you start having second thoughts on us," the other guy snapped. "It's bad enough that Frank had his major freak out on us regarding this."

Frank, Garret thought. *The guy guarding Gregg in the first place and who then moved him.*

"I still don't know what got to him about this guy."

"I don't know either," he said. "Frank's always been a bit of a fruit loop anyway. Especially since having his kid, and then his wife and kid took off on him."

"Yeah, but come on. That was clearly the smart thing for her to do."

Garret stood still in the closet and wondered about that. Had his brother managed to convince Frank that Gregg was a father and that his kid needed his father? If Gregg had any idea that his captor had that kind of a history, he might have played that card. Who wouldn't have?

Settling in to wait, Garret knew it was all about picking the right moment because, once they realized the women were gone, all hell would break loose. He didn't want to be the one taking the heat, but, if they all took off out of the house, that would be even better. Maybe he could pick up his brother and get him the hell away from here.

Again he studied his brother's condition, calculating if he could move on his own or if Garret would literally have to pick him up and carry him. His brother was six-two and an easy 240 pounds. He'd carry him if he had to, but it sure as hell wouldn't be easy, and he wouldn't get very far, very fast. It would be a lot better if Gregg could move on his own steam.

Just then the whining voice said, "You got any food in this place? We didn't even stop and get anything."

169

"But we're here now," the other man said, "so it's all good."

"Yeah, food's in the kitchen," the big man said. "Not much but probably something in the fridge, leftover pizza maybe."

"Perfect," the one guy said, as he scrambled into the kitchen. He came back with pizza, and, hearing absolutely nothing unusual, Garret frowned, wondering how long it would be before anybody realized the women were missing. The whiny guy kept eating pizza and talking about getting paid and what he would do with his money. The other guys didn't say anything, but Garret caught an odd look in the gaze of one of them. Garret wondered if the whiny dude had any idea that the chances were good that he wouldn't live to spend his money.

Why would they share three ways, when they could share only two? Garret had seen it happen time and time again. Once the gunmen realized how little their money would actually buy and what they had risked to get it, they thought about getting a bigger share of the pie. Garret was pretty damn sure that's what was going down, based on the one guy's gaze.

Just as he was about to put another bite of pizza in his mouth, the one guy Garret could barely see came up behind him and smacked him hard in the head. He crumpled to the ground, and there was immediate silence.

The big guy asked, "So did you mean to do that?"

"I wanted him to shut the fuck up," he said.

"Or are we talking about shutting him up permanently and not having to share with him?"

The other guy chuckled. "I knew you'd catch on pretty damn fast."

"Oh, I caught on," he said. "I just want to make sure you don't have any plans to treat me the same way."

"Like hell I would. Come on. We go way back."

"I remember, but I don't know where you found this pissant," he sneered. "Because he's definitely not somebody I want to listen to for long."

"Of course not. He's just a pain in the ass. That's what he is." He looked at the unconscious guy and said, "Another blow to the head? What do you think?"

"If you got a gun, use it," the big guy said.

"That would make a hell of a mess though. What I don't want to do is leave any trace of him."

"It's not our place," he said. "I'm not even sure who the hell's place this even is now."

"I thought you said it was yours?"

"Well, it was, but we didn't keep up the property tax, so who knows what happened then," he said. "I just knew that nobody was living here."

"Sweet," the other guy said.

"You're right though," he said. "Let's leave no trace."

"I hear you. Let's take him outside and then finish the job. Another blow to the head might do it better though."

"That's what I was thinking," the big guy said. He turned and watched the other guy, and there was that odd look in his gaze again.

Garret had unknowingly picked a wonderful spot to see this whole scene play out.

"Are we deep-sixing the guy who was lost, that we finally found again?" the big guy asked.

"I don't have any orders to do that," he said. "You can bet I won't take on a murder rap for the paltry money we're being paid."

"I know," he said. "That's why I was thinking of upping the money, just a little bit."

"I got no argument with that," he said. "I would do it just to shut up this whiny asshole." At that, he sniggered and picked up the lamp off to the side, took out the light bulb, and pulled back hard, slamming the unconscious man in the head. He hit him once, twice.

On the third blow, the big guy said, "Don't you think it's done?"

Garret noted how the big guy hadn't broken up, as he watched his unconscious coworker take multiple blows. But the big guy was watching the other guy carefully, as if wondering what the hell he was up to. You couldn't trust anybody who would pull a deal like that because, as soon as the other guy thought about splitting the money down from three to two, it was an easy jump to think about taking it all for himself.

The other guy nodded his head slightly and said, "Yeah, I should stop."

"I just didn't want to have too much blood around."

"Actually, that stayed fairly well contained," he said, with a half snort.

"Almost looks like you've done it a time or two," the big guy said.

"Only when I had to," he said. "With other losers, like this one."

The big guy just nodded and didn't say anything more.

Garret watched in shock, as they calmly cleaned up a little bit of splatter.

The big guy said, "Let's get this guy out to the front yard. If the women even see this, they'll freak out."

"Yeah, where are they anyway?"

"Oh, I'll take you to meet them," he said, "but let's get this guy out of here first." It didn't take much, and they picked up the dead man and carried him outside.

Immediately Garret skirted from his hiding spot and headed toward the kitchen. He needed a better hiding place because, once they got to the kitchen, that's when the shit would happen. The pantry would do. The fact that they had already removed one more of the guys was hugely helpful. He sent Kano another update, knowing it would be passed on to everybody else, as well.

Only the two bad guys didn't come back to the kitchen right away. Garret heard them drop onto the couches in the front room, gathered around Gregg. "Now where do we want to deep-six our former partner?" The killer laughed at his own words.

"Some marshland's not too far from here," the big guy said. "The center is really deep. We dump him in there, and he won't be found for quite a while."

"That works for me. You mind if I have some of that pizza he had?"

"Nope, I don't mind at all," he said.

The one guy hopped up and headed to the kitchen. But he heard sounds of the big man getting up and following. But quietly. Always wary, always on the hunt. Always alert.

"I hope he left us some," the one guy said, seemingly unaware of what he was up against. But anybody in this business already knew that you don't turn your back on somebody like that, and, in his case, you'd never let a guy, who had just killed your other partner, out of the room, where he could pull a gun and come back and take you out without a thought.

And, if Garret were ever in a situation like that, he

would try to do the same thing; that's exactly how he would make this work. A little scary to think about, but he watched and waited because the tableau in front of him could go any which way. But he knew one thing: it would all break loose very quickly.

CHAPTER 14

"WHY HASN'T GARRET said anything?" Astra asked Kano.

"He's said plenty," Kano said, hiding with them in the trees.

"Yes, but he hasn't said it's all clear, hasn't said we can come, hasn't said he needs you. Nothing!" She hated that sense of worry driving her.

"I know you're worried about him," he said, "but he will tell us what he can."

"Great," she muttered. "Do we know for sure nobody else is here?"

"No, I think Garret was expecting two men to be posted out here."

"And we don't know how many came in with them in the vehicle?" Astra asked him.

"Yes, we do," Kano answered patiently. "Listen. Just because you keep asking the same questions, it doesn't mean different answers will show up."

She groaned. "Sorry, it's an old habit."

"I get it," he said. "Most of the time, it wouldn't be an issue, but, right now, it's pissing me off, so would you mind?"

She grinned in the darkness. "No," she said. "I'm good."

"Why can't we just go home?" Amy said.

"What home is that?" Kano snapped. "The one you walked away from, where you were secure? We would all be doing much better right now, instead of sitting out here in the dark, after having to come after you." That shut up her sister, which surprised Astra, but maybe Amy finally understood some of what she'd brought on.

"But, if Garret's in there," Astra said, "he'll need help. You need to go help him."

"I need to make sure you two are safe," he said. "If you weren't here with us, or if we hadn't found Amy at the same time, I would be in there, but we can't afford that. So our resources are a little thin."

"So then let me go," Astra said quietly.

He snorted.

She looked at him balefully. "I was a help last time."

"Beginner's luck," he snapped back, and then he held up a finger.

She shushed immediately and turned to look. Indeed, somebody was walking around. He held a rifle over his shoulder, completely unsuspecting of anybody being out here. She wondered if he was really that stupid or if he just really thought nothing was going on. As she watched, Kano looked at her, motioned for her to stay with her sister, then disappeared into the shadows. She sank back into the darkness. "There is just no end to these bad guys," she murmured.

Amy wrapped her arms around Astra and held on.

Touched, and for the first time maybe understanding where her sister was coming from, she hugged her back.

Amy whispered, "I'm sorry."

She nodded against her sister's hair. "I know," she said.

"I sure wish I had stayed where I was supposed to. I'm

also sorry about Garret," she said. "I knew it was all wrong, right from the beginning."

"So why did you stay with him?" Astra asked.

She shrugged. "I don't know. He was a force to be dealt with. I just didn't know how."

"And is Gregg any easier?"

"Very, and he treats me differently."

"No, he treats you more like a porcelain doll," she said. "Whereas, Garret treated you as a partner."

"Yet he knew I wasn't a partner. I was always inferior in his eyes."

"I don't know about that," she said.

"Oh, I do," she snapped. "He had that look that said I just wasn't quite what he wanted me to be, like he was always disappointed in me."

Astra didn't have anything to say about that because she could possibly understand it. Her sister was always one of those who looked after herself instead of the good of both. "Hopefully your relationship with Gregg is a little easier."

"Easier, maybe," she said. "But sure as hell not better in that sense of them treating me like I'm stupid at times."

"These are very capable men," Astra said. "You have to give them some leeway." She held her sister in her arms, and the two of them just rocked back and forth in the darkness. She listened for any kind of sound, but there was only silence, with an occasional twig crackling here and there, or a leaf would fall and catch her eye. A bird would call somewhere in the darkness, and it all just grated on her nerves, as the tension wound up tighter and tighter. She squeezed her arms, until Amy protested.

"Sorry," she whispered. "I wish Kano was back."

Suddenly he was there, carrying another man. He slowly

lowered him to the ground, next to the other unconscious man that he'd taken out earlier. He pulled something from his back pocket and quickly tied up the second man as well. He looked at the two women and asked, "Are you guys okay?"

"We are," Astra said. "We just want all this over with."

"Got it," he said. "I heard from Garret. Gregg is in the house. Three men as well, and they just took out one of their own."

"Oh, shit," Astra said, staring at him. "What does that mean?"

"It's quite possible that there'll be another argument coming up, so he's warning me to stay here, on the chance that the numbers may drop by one more, and then he'll only have the one in there to deal with."

"That's not very smart of them, is it?"

"That depends. If it's one paycheck to be split—"

She winced at that. "And, if there's greed among those two gunmen, they'll probably try to take each other out."

"What about these two?" Amy stared at the two guards on the ground.

"That's another issue," he said. "These two men might have gotten killed, once they went back up to the house, completely unsuspecting of what's really going on."

"Wow, nice world," Amy whispered.

"Not much of it," Kano said. "It definitely has good parts to it, but also a lot of parts are pretty shitty." He held up his phone and said, "I'm just waiting for Garret to tell us which way he wants us to go. I've told him that we have both of the guards."

Just then a shot came from inside the house.

Astra stared at Kano. "Oh, God," she said. "Please tell

me that's not Garret."

He looked at the phone grimly and shrugged. "I won't know," he said, "until somebody contacts me."

"We have to go in," Astra said, bolting to her feet.

He reached out and grabbed her arm, his hand firm. "No, we're not doing that," he said. "Because, if Garret's still hidden, barging in there will only let them know he's there. We're waiting. That's the only thing we can do right now."

THE SHOT CAME out of nowhere.

Garret froze and realized the killer had taken a bullet. From Garret's new hiding spot in the pantry, he barely caught sight of anything but the two guys' hands, and he saw a handgun falling. He whistled silently. So it was just as he'd thought. The killer had used the pizza as a ruse to go to the kitchen to grab a moment, so he could turn the tables on the big guy. Why split the money at all, if he could keep it all for himself?

The big man stood over the other one and fired a second shot, right into his head.

"Fucking double-crossing fucking bastard." And that just started his rant. He kept on, until his temper wore down. Finally he looked up and groaned. "Now I got two bodies to deal with." Then he pulled out his phone and sent a message. When no response came within a few minutes, he sent another one. "Where the fuck are they now? What's the fucking point of having sentries, if they don't fucking answer when you need them? They're probably sleeping in the goddamn underbrush," he snapped. He picked up the dead guy and hauled him out the front door.

Garret sent a message to Kano. **It's now the two of us**

against him.

Just as he was about to leave the pantry, the big man came back, running at top speed. He headed into the kitchen with a wild look in his eyes and started screaming at the top of his lungs, "Fuck, fuck, fuck, where are you goddamn bitches?" He reached down, found the ropes, saw the cut edges, and something dark and sinister came over his face. "Goddammit," he said. "If it isn't bad enough to have betrayal from within, now I have to deal with betrayal from the outside. Some assholes came and took the women. What are the chances that he got the sentries too?" He stared outside, a glare, deep and dark, on his face.

"What the fuck." He turned to look at Gregg, who was still out cold on the couch. He walked over and gave him a hard shake. Gregg groaned. "Wake up," the big guy said. "Wake the fuck up." Gregg opened blurry eyes and then groaned. He closed his eyes again. "Oh no, you don't," he said. "I need answers from you."

"I don't ... have any answers," Gregg muttered.

"Who would come to your rescue?"

He gave a hard laugh. "Nobody," he said. "I fucked over everybody in my life who counts, and anybody who still cares is incapable."

"Well, I had your goddamn girlfriend here," he said, "as a prisoner to hand over with you. Now she's gone, along with her damn sister. And that sister is just a no-good little bitch, and I bet she's behind all this shit," he said. "I should've shot her right from the beginning, when I realized what she was like."

Gregg stared up at him uncomprehendingly, as if it was all just too much, then slumped backward again. Immediately the big guy started to swear again, and he pulled out his phone and made a call. "You come get him, and you come get him now," he said. "Everything's gone to shit, and I want this guy out of here."

He listened to whoever was speaking on the other end.

"Don't you fucking talk to me about those women," he said. "You come get this asshole, before I don't give you that opportunity anymore." With that, he slammed his phone down on the coffee table. He strode back to the kitchen, threw open the back door, and yelled out into the woods, "Come and get me, you little pissant," he said. "You think I'll let a little pissant like you ruin everything?" He returned inside and slammed the door as hard as he could.

After that rampage, Garret wondered if he should just take him out. But what he needed were the people coming to pick up his brother. And that transaction was something Garret couldn't allow them to complete, but Garret still needed the big guy to start the exchange. So Garret couldn't take the big guy out just yet.

Garret sent a message to Kano, telling him that he needed backup. Only the one big guy was left, and they needed to move to set up a sting for the people coming to collect his brother. He got an affirmative response and settled in to wait. They would need some distraction in order to get the upper hand here. This guy was no fool now, and he was on high alert and edgy as hell. He would be trigger-happy, and anybody who got in his line of fire would go down. Garret just had to make sure it wasn't him or any of the people he had with him. Neither woman could handle the kind of damage this guy could inflict, and, if Garret lost Kano, well, this guy would pay in a big way.

CHAPTER 15

"**W**HAT'S GOING ON?" Astra murmured. Kano filled her in. "How will you do that?" she asked.

"We need a distraction," he said, just as they watched the house door thrown open.

He roared, "Send that bitch back in here, or I'll kill the boyfriend."

Amy gasped, and Astra froze at that. "Is he likely to?"

"Hell yeah, he's likely to, but we also have to remember that Garret's in there."

"Sure," Astra said, "but he can fire anytime and not let this guy take out Gregg."

"Garret could also take several gunshots himself," he said.

"Right, so the best thing is for me to go in," Astra said. "It's me who the gunman's pissed at."

He looked at her in shock, and her sister cried out, "No!" she said. "You can't do that."

"Yes, I can," Astra said, hopping to her feet. "And I still have that handgun."

He thought about it and said, "It could get ugly."

"It already is ugly," she said. "The trouble is, I need to know my sister will stay out of this." She turned to look at Amy, but she was curled up and shuddering in fear. "I mean it, Amy. No more backstabbing, no more lying or telling me that you'll do one thing and then go sneaking out the door."

Amy just glared at her. "But you'll get killed."

"Yeah, well, in that case, maybe you'll do a better job raising your child. If I'm not around, maybe it'll be a reminder to you to do the best you can." She looked at Kano and said, "I'll walk across. You take your time setting up, so you know that you've got this big guy, so you have Garret covered."

"Yeah," he said. "You know what'll happen when Garret finds out what you've done."

She chuckled. "Yeah, he'll be pissed. But you can deal with it."

He just shook his head. "Maybe you don't know him that well."

"No, but I understand the kind of guy he is," she said. "He'll be pissed." She got up and walked across the yard, calling out, "Don't hurt him."

The big man stood there, his hands on his hips. "Where's the other one?"

"Lost in the darkness," she snapped. "She took off on me."

"Well, it's betrayal everywhere around here right now," he said.

"Well, what did you expect me to do?" she sneered. "Not try to escape?"

"Honestly it makes sense that you did," he said. "But hats off to you for succeeding. Of course it just made me more pissed off than usual, and I'm really looking forward to beating the shit out of you for that."

Her steps faltered, and he nodded with satisfaction. "You better be afraid, bitch," he snapped. "You'll pay for what you just did."

"I didn't do anything," she said. "We just ran out of the kitchen."

"How the hell did you even get a knife?"

"What are you talking about?" she said. "You left it on the kitchen counter."

He stopped, nonplussed. Then he shrugged. "Maybe I did," he said, and, as soon as she got up on the porch, he grabbed her roughly and dragged her into the living room.

She dropped down beside Gregg and checked his pulse. "What did you do to him?" she cried out. But, inside, she was absolutely delighted to see him.

"Doesn't matter what we did," he said. "It's what we're still doing."

She glared at him. "Like what?"

"Don't you worry," he snarled. "This deal's finally going down."

Then she saw the blood on the floor. "Jesus!" she said. "What the hell did you do in here?"

"I didn't do anything. You remember that."

"Well, blood's all over the floor, so obviously you did something," she snapped.

"One of my team decided to backstab me," he said, with a growl. "That's what happens to betrayers."

"Right," she said. "Can't blame you there. I feel the same way."

He seemed somewhat mollified. "Get him to wake up," he snapped, "before I come charging in with all kinds of ways to make him wake up."

She reached over and gently shook Gregg's shoulder. "Gregg, are you there?" He just moaned. "Jesus," she said. "Did you guys pistol whip him or something?"

"Or something, but it wasn't me. He just got here. Remember?"

She glared at him, not sure where the hell Garret was but trusting that the guys had her back. She said, "So now what? You have all the money for yourself?"

"Hell no," he said. "Two more guys are outside."

She stared at him in astonishment. "What? I didn't see any guys outside."

He nodded. "Yeah, that's what I'm wondering about too."

He looked at her intently, but she just shook her head. "I didn't see anybody," she said.

He started to swear. "Goddammit, if those two little pissants took off, I'll come after them and make them darn sorry for leaving me like that."

"Maybe they saw you kill that guy, the backstabber, and they didn't want any part of it."

He stood here, his eyes closed, his hands on his hips, as if thinking it through, and then nodded. "And that's probably exactly what happened." He brightened at that. "But then again, I don't have to pay them, so that's all good."

"Did you even get a paycheck?" she said, with a half smile.

"No, they're on their way. Right now. So payday is coming."

She stared at him in shock.

He nodded. "You didn't think you would get out of this unscathed, did you?"

"Well, I'd hoped so," she said, sagging onto the couch. Just as she wondered what she should do, Gregg gently squeezed her hand. She let out a slow deep breath and squeezed his fingers back. What she needed to know for certain was what this big guy knew or to be sure that he didn't have any clue.

She looked at the bully. "And when they come, then what?"

"Then you and him will get hauled out of here, and I'll get paid, and I'm leaving," he said. "Before any more shit goes wrong."

"And the blood and wherever the bodies are that you've got stashed here?"

He snorted. "I can't go out and deal with them right now," he said. "So I'll make it a part of the deal, for them to take care of."

"If you say so," she said, frowning. "But what if they won't pay you, when they see the mess you made?"

He just glared at her, but she could see that she'd gotten him thinking.

"Shit," he said. Just then came the sound of a vehicle coming up the road.

She looked at him. "Well, guess you'll find out soon enough because it looks like we've got company."

"Oh, yeah, we got company all right," he said, with a big smirk. "And you'll finally get what's coming to you."

She glared at him. "I haven't done anything to you. I don't know why you've got such hate for me."

"I hate all bitches," he said. "Ones with brains are the worst."

She looked at him, smiled, and said, "Thank you, that was an obvious compliment. I knew you didn't hate me."

"It wasn't meant that way," he snapped.

She shrunk. "It doesn't matter. I'll take it anyway."

Just then the vehicle pulled up into the driveway, and the lights shone on the house. He walked toward the front door, then stopped and looked at her hesitantly.

"Where am I going?" she asked. "I already came back."

"No, I can't believe that. Not the way things are going tonight." He walked back over beside her and hit her hard in the side of the head. She collapsed onto the couch without another word.

SWEARING HEAVILY AT that little scenario, Garret waited until the big guy headed out the front door. Then he raced into the living room. He said to Gregg, "Wake the hell up." Then Garret picked up Astra and carried her out to the back porch, returning once more to the front room.

Gregg said, "I'm here. I'm here."

Garret shoved the handgun Astra had kept in the back of her waistband, under her jacket, to Gregg. "Now that she's safely out of the way, we need to get all of them."

Gregg, keeping up with the headlights still shining in the front, stood, a little wobbly at first, then said, "Come on. Let's go."

They immediately stood on either side of the front door, hidden by the old thick ornate curtains covering the windows on each side.

Outside, yelling was going on.

"I guess they found the bodies," Garret noted.

"What the fuck, man," the one guy said. "We can't deal with these bodies."

"It's not my fucking fault," the big guy said. "The first one was his bullshit because he didn't want to share, and he wanted whiny guy to just shut the hell up. Then the fucker pulled a gun on me, so I had to take him out. What the hell? Do you think I would stand here and get myself shot?"

"I don't know," he said. "This is all bullshit."

"Maybe so, but, if you want your prisoners, come get them," he snapped. "They're on the couch. The girl too."

"The girlfriend?"

"No, the girlfriend's sister."

"Well then, we're not paying you full price. You didn't fully deliver," he said.

"You're paying me full price," he said. "I had the girl-friend. I went through too much for this."

"We wanted the girlfriend, not the sister," he said. "Anybody with brains would know that."

"Well, with these two prisoners, you can get the other one."

But, as far as Garret and Gregg could see, the one guy was backing up toward the car. "No, you clean up this shit first."

"You get the hell in here and get your prisoners," the big guy roared. "Otherwise I'll release Gregg and the girl. And then you can deal with whatever."

The new arrival had a conversation with somebody on the driver's side. "Fine, I'm coming in to get him," he said. "But I want you to step out first. No way you'll shoot me, like you shot your brother."

"Oh, no. No way," he said. "You owe me some money. Until I get my money, I'm not giving you nothing."

"You told me to come get him," he said, exasperated.

"Well, I've already seen too much tonight," he said. "This can go down easy, or it can go down seriously ugly."

"Well then, ugly it is." The guy dropped to the ground.

With that, the driver reached out of the car window and fired twice. The big man stood in shock, getting hit once in the arm and once in the leg, and then he roared and started toward the one man still outside the vehicle.

"Fuck, shoot him again, shoot him again," screamed the man outside the car. "Jesus Christ, this is a shitstorm. Kill him."

Two more shots were fired, hitting the big man in the torso, and he stopped and swayed in place. The final two shots did him in, and he fell flat, facedown on the ground.

Garret and Gregg looked at each other, as the vehicle stayed where it was. "Now what we need," Garret said, "is for these two last guys standing to come in and get you."

"But will they? It looks like a trap. What are the chances that they'll just leave us and run?"

"The one guy's on the phone." They watched as he paced back and forth, swearing and cussing into the phone. They couldn't hear the words, but it was pretty easy to read his body language.

Finally he walked around to the driver. "We're supposed to leave it all," he said. "Call the cops and bring them in, but make sure that Gregg's dead too."

"Then go do it," the driver said.

"Shit," he said. "It looks like a goddamn trap to me."

"Stop being such a wuss," the one guy yelled, as the other man walked slowly toward the front door. "Well then, I'm coming in behind you, as backup."

"At least we got paid already. Not only that but we've also got the money we were supposed to pay these guys." The first man, closest to the house, turned and said, "We still have to kill Gregg. If we don't shoot him, you know they'll come back on us."

"No, go shoot him, put him down, take out the girl too," he said. "Then we can get the hell out of here."

He walked into the house, and immediately Gregg

grabbed him and pulled him to the side. He held a gun to his head, then Garret fired his gun once and then a second time into the floor. Then Gregg said, "How about you head back out there to your buddy?"

The guy just looked at Gregg in shock, bolted out the front door, and met with two more gunshots from the driver. The one man they had just tagged, fell facedown, dead. The other man, now in the vehicle, ripped out backward, while they raced toward the car, but it was gone in the darkness.

"Goddammit," Gregg said, limping badly as they stopped.

"Yeah, you've got a bit of talking to do," Garret said.

"Yeah, you're not kidding," he said. "What a fucking mess."

"You want to tell me what the hell's going on here?"

"Well, I can tell you some of it," he said, "but it's kind of shitty."

"What's that?"

"They were trying to use me as a patsy for taking down your plane, realizing that we'd had a split over Amy. They would use that to make it look like I was trying to get rid of you permanently."

Garret stared at his brother. "I guess they don't understand brothers, do they?"

With that, he could see some of the stiffness and the stress in Gregg's shoulders ease back. "Thank you," he said. "I was afraid you wouldn't believe me."

"There's a lot in life I believe," he said, "and there are shitty things in life you've done to me, but I didn't ever think that you would have done that."

"And yet, for many people," Gregg said, still wary, "they would think that moving from screwing your girlfriend to killing you isn't that big of a step."

"Yeah, maybe so," he said. "So the next time you decide you'll go knock up one of my girlfriends, I suggest you make sure that we're done first."

"Shit, man. I've loved her since forever."

"She's bad news for me, and I shouldn't have anything to do with her, but really? … You couldn't have just told me that you loved her?"

"I should have. I know. But it was a stolen weekend, and then, after we fought, she left. She went back to you, when she was supposed to go home to break up with you and to come back with me, but she didn't. She went back to you instead and stayed there. Until I couldn't stay away, and you caught us."

"Yeah, nothing's terribly straightforward about Amy."

"Will you forgive me for that ever?"

"Yeah, but only for two reasons," he said. "Believe me. I'll never forget it because that's just a shitty thing to do to your brother. And it's been eating away at me for a long time."

His brother winced at that. "So what are the two reasons?"

"First, Amy and I would have been an absolute disaster of a relationship," he said. "I can't stand anybody without any guts or grit. And, second, because her sister and I will be an item, whether Astra knows it yet or not."

At that, Gregg stared at him in surprise. "Seriously?"

"Yeah," he said.

Gregg started to laugh. "You know what? That's the best thing ever," he said affectionately. "I told Amy that the two of you would be great together a long time ago. She told me that I was off my rocker and that it would never happen."

"Well, with any luck, it's already happened," he said. "It's just that we've spent the last however many shitty days trying to find you." He helped his brother back into the house. "We've got a hell of a mess here to deal with now too."

"Not only do we have a hell of a mess," he said, "but we still don't know who's behind that attack on the plane. And it wasn't me, dude. I swear to God. It wasn't me."

"So who the hell was it then?" Garret snapped.

"Somebody needs to have a talk and, I mean, a forceful talk, with Deedee. I don't know that she's behind it, but she sure as hell knows more than she's letting on."

"She's such a bitch," Garret said.

"Yeah, she's also one of Bullard's exes too. You know that, right?"

"So what? Or are you thinking a woman scorned and all that?"

"It's possible," Gregg said. "It's definitely possible."

"But then it's not just Deedee, is it?"

"No, it isn't, but I don't know who all has been carrying a torch all this time."

"Goddamn relationships," Garret said. "Gets you in trouble every damn time." After he helped Gregg back into the house, Garret walked straight through the house and out to where Astra was lying on the back porch.

She opened her eyes, as he approached. "That guy's got a hand like a sledgehammer."

"I saw you pull back, ever-so-slightly, before you took the hit."

She grinned at him. "Yeah, I was taught that in self-defense."

"Good," he said. "But, Jesus, what a hit." He helped her

to her feet and folded her into his arms. She snuggled in deep, and, over her shoulder, he looked at his brother and raised an eyebrow. His brother grinned.

"I'm really glad to see this," Gregg said.

She twisted in Garret's arms. "Gregg, how are you doing?"

"I feel like shit," he said. "I'll definitely need some x-rays and some downtime. But I've been trying to convince my brother that I had nothing to do with what happened to him in the exploding plane."

"Pretty sure he believes you," she said, then coolly added, "once he got over the anger of what you really did to him."

He looked at her, frowned, and then nodded. "Yeah, you're right. I can see you know how he would feel about it."

"Yeah, that kind of shit? It tends to travel," she said, with a half smile.

"Well, he's forgiven me, and it's better off for you now."

"Absolutely," she said, "but that doesn't mean it was the way to go about it."

He just groaned. "Please, ... no more lectures. I feel like shit already," he said, as he slowly sank to the floor in front of them.

At that, Garret tugged her back into his arms and kissed her soundly.

CHAPTER 16

AFTER THAT, KANO and Amy joined in their reunion, while multiple phone calls were made to Charles, waiting for Jonas to show up, expecting his fury when he saw the mess around them. Garret's apology was a little tongue-in-cheek for having caused such chaos. An ambulance arrived for Gregg, and Kano and Amy went along to ensure Gregg made it there safely. Astra stood with Garret among all the chaos, close to his side. When things had finally calmed down a bit, she looked at him and asked, "Can we leave soon?"

"I think so," he said, "but I don't know that we'll be allowed to leave the country just yet."

"That's fine." she said, "but a bed would be very nice."

He looked at her and raised an eyebrow.

She chuckled. "I'm not one to jump into bed that fast."

"How fast is fast?" he asked. "You've been holding a torch for me for a long time now."

She stared at him in shock.

"Hey, I was just teasing," he said, reaching out and sneaking her back into his arms.

"The trouble is," she said, "it's true."

He stared at her in surprise.

"Ever since you first set out to be with Amy," she said, "I kept hoping you'd break up. But then, the way she did it, I

195

knew it would take a long time for you to get over it and to not be bitter. I really hated her myself for a while then," she said, with half a smile. "Because she ruined my chance at happiness too. I figured you'd never look at me without thinking of her and what she'd done."

"Wow," he said. "I told my brother that one of the reasons I forgave him was because he saved me from what was bound to be a terrible relationship with Amy and that it left the pathway open for me to have one with you."

"Which we should have done a long time ago," she said, poking him in the chest.

"That just brings me back to that point, about how long we've already been waiting," he said, with a leer.

She smiled. "How about we just go grab some sleep and then see how we feel? Besides, my face is killing me."

At that, he nodded and kissed her tenderly, saying, "You're right. Let me get the okay from Jonas to get the hell out of here." He got the okay, and they left in a vehicle driven by one of Jonas's guys. Soon they were back at Charles's home, where he opened the door for them. He took one look at her face and started clucking like a mother hen.

"It's not that bad," she said but winced when he gently put an ice pack up against her cheek. "Okay, so it's not that good either."

"A harsh blow like that can take a while to heal, my dear," he said. "Tomorrow it's likely to be real pretty."

She groaned. "In other words, I won't want to go out in public for a while."

"Nope, not unless you want to explain to everybody that this guy didn't beat you up."

"I'd never do that," Garret said.

"I know that," she said, "but everybody else won't know that."

Charles led them to their rooms and said good night. She didn't even know what time it was, and she didn't care. She crashed onto her bed and was almost asleep, when a knock came at the door. "Come in," she said.

Garret walked in, wearing only his boxers, then pulled back the bedding on the other side and said, "Go to sleep."

"What are you doing?" she murmured.

"I decided that I came too close to losing a lot tonight," he said. "I don't want to lose anymore. So I'll just hold you and keep you safe."

She protested, shifting up on one arm to look at him.

"Maybe we can have a little private time later, after you get some sleep."

She groaned. "Listen. You couldn't have saved me from getting hit in the face, and you know I came back to the house on my own."

"Yeah, I know," he said, and his tone fully indicated how he felt about that choice.

"I'd do it again too," she said. "It was the diversion you needed, and it was what we had to do to get to the bottom of this. Or closer to the bottom of this."

"Well, I just want to know right now that you're safe."

"So, what you mean is that you just want to sleep, and you wanted me beside you," she murmured, with a note of laughter in her voice.

"Absolutely," he said. "So take it easy on an old man. I've been through a lot tonight."

She smiled, snuggled in deep, and said, "Not a problem. I agree. We've both been through a lot." With his arms wrapped around her, laying nestled together, spoon style, they settled in.

She tossed and turned, as she wasn't used to sleeping with somebody. But, in the wee hours, she crashed long and deep. When she woke up, it was to a sense of well-being and rest. But, when she rolled over, her face was puffy and sore. She groaned slightly.

"Take it easy," he said. "You're good. It's all okay."

"My face," she said. Opening her eyes, unsurprised to see him there, she smiled. "I must look quite the sight."

"You're beautiful," he said. "I remember that one of the mistakes I made with your sister early on was when I told her how beautiful you were. She didn't appreciate it."

She gave him a wry smile. "You should never tell a woman that another woman is beautiful; especially when it's her sister."

He smiled. "I made a lot of mistakes with her, and I'm hoping not to make the same ones with you."

"You won't," she said. "I won't let you."

With a shout of laughter, he pulled her close into his arms. She rolled against him, feeling such a sense of rightness and balance in her life and joy at being in his arms. She snaked her arms around his neck and said, "Now what was that conversation we had last night?"

He leaned over and nuzzled her nose with his. "I think it had something to do with sharing some private time."

"Now sounds like the perfect private time to me."

"Well, Charles might call us to breakfast."

"Nah, he's a wise old bird," she said. "He knows exactly what's going on."

He chuckled and said, "Will it bother you?"

"What? People knowing I'm having a relationship with my sister's ex?"

"Yeah."

"No," she said. "It won't bother me. Will it bother you?"

"Nope," he said. "I'm truly past all that."

"Well, I'm glad to hear that," she said, reaching up to kiss him gently. "Because I've waited a long time for this."

"You were serious?"

"Very," she said. "It broke my heart when I realized the two of you were engaged. It just was so wrong, when I knew all along you were so right for me. And there was absolutely nothing I could do. My relationship with my sister was already on the tenuous side. How could I tell her that she couldn't have you, when you two were already engaged? I cried myself to sleep many a night."

He winced at that. "I wasn't very smart apparently," he said. "I couldn't see what was right in front of me."

"I don't think you're alone in that," she said, with a smile. "That's the complaint a lot of people have. You know—hindsight's 20/20 and all."

"I hear you there," he said, with a gentle smile. He leaned over, kissed her, and said, "So we have a lot of time to make up for."

"You think so, huh? But I'm not in any hurry, and I don't want to rush through it. I want to savor every moment."

"That sounds perfect for me," he murmured. "It's been a long time since I was happy."

"Well, I suggest that joy becomes our new word of the year," she said. "Let's try to find joy somehow, in every day."

"All this is still not over. You know that, right?"

"I know," she said. "It's not over. You guys still need to find out exactly what happened to the plane you were in. And who hated you so much that they would be waging war on your team. But, for the moment, you've done enough."

"I'm not sure," he said. "But we'll find out from Kano what's going on and what they've done since they've been out all night. He'll need to pick up that conversation with Deedee too," he murmured. "And then I should go, as backup."

"Maybe you should," she said agreeably. "Or maybe somebody else should."

He frowned at that.

"Are there just the two of you now?"

He shook his head. "No," he said, "a few others are on our team."

"So maybe, instead of being the hero all the time," she said, "you should let somebody else step in and do a leg of this nastiness too."

"We'll see," he compromised.

She chuckled out loud. "I think that means, *Hell no.* Am I right?"

"No," he said, "it doesn't. But it does mean that I'm thinking about my life. You know? And what I need to do to make a little more joy happen."

"Well then, how about we start here and now?" she whispered, reaching up to kiss him.

He lowered his head, giving her a deep drunken kiss that fired her senses all at once.

When he lifted his head, she murmured, "Wow, I didn't realize just how potent your kiss would be."

"I know. Yours too," he said, his voice thick. "And, now that I have you in my arms, it's all I can think about." And he lowered his head again and again and again. Each time lifting his head and trying to control himself, before going back down, like a drunk man, wanting another drink.

This time she held him close and wouldn't let him raise his head. Passion spiked between them, and their bodies twisted sinuously against each other, both of them only in underwear, she without even a bra.

She rolled over on top of him, dropping kisses on his lips and his nose, across his face. She clasped his head, so that she could stare down at his beloved features. "I've missed you," she said.

He nodded and said, "And I missed you. I just didn't even know how much or that you were even there for me. I wish we hadn't wasted all that time."

"It makes this time now seem all the sweeter," she murmured. Again she lowered her head and kissed him gently.

"If you say so," he murmured. "I'll spend a lot of time making it up to you."

She smiled. "I'll never say no to that."

He chuckled, then he flipped her over, under him, as he said, "You're injured, so maybe you should just lie there and rest."

"I'm not that injured," she said drily.

Then he worked his way down her body, gently caressing and loving every inch of her. Almost as if he thought that having missed so much, he wouldn't miss one inch more. By the time he reached her pelvic bone, she was twisting madly on the bed, crying out for him.

"Oh no," he said. "You won't have it that easy."

She groaned. "Easy?" she gasped. "I want you so much."

"And I want you too," he said. "But I want to make sure this is all about you."

"No," she ordered. "This is about us."

He slowly worked his way up, his fingers sliding underneath her panties, and, the next thing she knew, they were gone. And somehow he disposed of his boxers and was sliding between her thighs.

She opened up, eagerly, his fingers teasing the moisture waiting for him. She groaned, as his fingers drove her crazy, pulling him to her, so she could kiss him. "Now," she demanded.

"Are you sure?" he murmured, sliding one finger inside, testing the width and breadth of her.

"Now," she moaned, lifting herself against his fingers.

He shifted, and suddenly there he was, and, with one swift movement, he was buried right to the heart of her.

She groaned, shudders rippling up and down her body, as she slightly adjusted her position to ease the size of him. "It's been a while," she gasped.

"Am I hurting you?"

"God no," she said "It feels wonderful. Don't you dare leave."

He chuckled. "I don't think I could," he said. "That would be a little too much to expect from my sense of control and all."

"Good," she murmured. "Do what you can do then," she added, tilting her hips, as he started moving.

He gave a slight sigh of pleasure, as he raised himself up on his elbows, then plunged, first slowly, and then deeper.

He slowly built momentum, until she was crying beneath him, and, when she came apart, all she heard was the groan of his own release, after having done the gentlemanly thing, letting the lady go first.

When she could finally breathe again, she said, "Next time, you get to go first."

"Hell no," he said, still gasping for breath. "You almost killed me already, so that'll never be a good thing."

"Oh, I think so," she moaned. "But you'll have to give me a minute to catch my breath."

He said, "I'll need a little more than a minute."

She smiled, then slid her hand down his torso and over his hips, to the thick coarse hair between his legs, only to find him already stirring. "Oh, is that right?" she asked.

He stared at her in shock, looked down at her hand, and said, "Well, that's never happened."

She snorted. "Well then," she said, "how about a replay—in a few minutes?"

"How about a replay right now?" he said, shifting onto his back, underneath her.

She smiled and said, "Sounds good to me." Then she straddled him, and, in a slow and deep rocking motion, she slowly took them both up to the edge, as the initial passion had already taken the edge off, and the slow gentle loving followed. One that she loved, just as much as the one before. The resulting climax they shared was just as powerful in its own way. When she finally slid down across his chest, breathless and gasping for air, she whispered, "Is it okay if I go back to sleep again?"

"I sure hope so," he said. "I'm already there ahead of you." With that, he tucked his arms around her, and the two of them fell back asleep.

She had a smile on her face, dreaming about the days to come.

EPILOGUE

K ANO LEFT THE hospital, after having spent quite a bit of time talking to Gregg, and made his way back to Charles's house.

Charles smiled at him. "I'd say it's been a good day, but you look pretty angry."

"We didn't get the car," he said. "And nobody's been able to track it. Jonas said he's got a team on it, but he's pissed."

"Oh, dear," Charles replied. "Now what?"

"I'll go see that bitch," he said.

"Not alone," Charles warned Kano.

"Well, it's not what I want to do, and I think backup would help, but I don't want to take Garret. He needs to spend some time with Astra and his brother. A bunch of healing needs to go on there with Amy too."

"And?" Charles said. "That doesn't mean you go alone."

Just then a knock came from the other side of the dividing wall. "You expecting company?" Kano asked, puzzled.

Charles nodded. "I am, indeed." He opened the door, and Fallon stepped through.

Kano looked at his buddy in surprise, then reached out and hugged him, hard. "Damn good to see you," he said. "We could have used you these last few days."

"I was on my way already," Fallon said, "when I heard

205

all the updates from Charles. I'm glad I'm here. We've filled in Ice and Blanchard too. Still no progress on the hunt for Bullard yet, unfortunately." He looked from one to the other. "So where are we going next?"

Kano looked at him in surprise, then at Charles, and asked, "Did you arrange this?"

Charles smiled and said, "I cannot tell a lie."

Kano chuckled and said, "Well, it's good that you're here, Fallon, and your timing is perfect."

"You haven't told me where we're going yet," Fallon said.

"First stop, Paris," Kano said.

"The bitch Deedee, who's always been after Bullard?" Fallon stopped, paused, and said, "Now that's an interesting concept."

"The question is whether she hates him enough to do something like this," Kano said.

"I wouldn't have said so," Fallon said slowly. "But I do agree, it's time we go find out. The team is running out of avenues to follow. You keep giving us new ones, but everything comes down to a dead end."

"Except for Deedee," Charles said. "If nothing else, you need to go knock her off the list." He looked at Kano and asked, "Did you get any sleep yet?"

"No," he said. "I need to crash and burn for a bit."

"I could use some rest too actually," Fallon said. "The flights were not great for that."

Charles looked at his watch and said, "It's almost midnight now. How about we have some food, a nightcap, and then you can both get a good night's sleep and leave in the morning."

The men agreed with that, and Fallon turned and asked,

"Where's Garret?"

At that, both men chuckled.

Fallon looked at them, surprised, and asked, "What's so funny?"

"He's in bed."

"Garret's in bed?"

"Yeah, but not alone."

At that, Fallon's eyebrows slowly climbed. "Amy?" he asked in shock.

"No, hell no, not Amy," Kano said. "Amy's sister. Astra."

Fallon looked at him in surprise, and Kano smiled and said, "This is a good thing."

"She's okay?" he asked hesitantly.

"Astra's a good person," he said. "She saved our ass, shot a couple bad guys in the process, and didn't even turn a hair. She took a punch in the face too because Gregg was still a prisoner and would get shot, if somebody didn't show up and diffuse the gunman's anger."

"Is she okay?" Fallon asked in alarm.

"She's more than okay. She's even better now. She apparently has loved Garret since he hooked up with Amy."

"Jesus," he said. "If only Garret had seen the right sister back then."

"History could be well rewritten on hindsight," Charles said. "Now let's get some food. We'll leave those two alone to rest up and to heal, on many levels," he said firmly. "If you want to talk to them, we'll do that at breakfast."

"Hell no," Kano said. "We need to be gone, before they're even up."

Fallon looked at him in surprise. "Why?"

"Otherwise Garret will insist on coming," he said.

"No, I'm here for this leg of the journey," Fallon said. "It's my turn to get into the nitty-gritty of this investigation. It's frustrating as hell being on the outside, trying to give suggestions, but not actually being here. Garret jumped back in way too early, considering the major head injury he got when the plane went down."

"Exactly why I called you," Charles said, as he led the way to the kitchen. Indeed, a perfectly browned pot roast sat on the counter, with its juices just settling in. The roasted veggies and gravy were also kept warm on the stovetop.

"How the hell did you even know that he was coming right now?" Kano asked Charles.

"Obviously," Charles said, "because I arranged it. Now let's eat!" After two minutes to dish up the plates, they sat down to eat and began to discuss the nightmare of Deedee.

Fallon stopped eating, halfway through his roast, stared, and said, "Wait, Kano. Wasn't there something about you and Deedee?"

"Oh, hell no," he said forcibly. "Deedee's like thirty years my senior. She was also sweet on Bullard, not that he cared."

"I thought something was there though," Fallon said, concentrating, as if trying to remember.

Charles looked at him and smiled. "Not a daughter by any chance, was it?"

"Fine, there was something," Kano said, glaring. "But it was just a minor something, with Deedee's daughter."

At that, Fallon started to laugh and laugh. "Oh, God," he said, "this is awesome. Wait until Ice finds out."

"Ice doesn't need to find out."

"Yes, she does, my boy," Charles said, as he looked at him and smiled. "She already knows. I contacted the group there this morning, looking for Bailey's cinnamon bun recipe. So, when I called, I filled in Ice on everything that just happened."

"Damn it, Charles," Kano said, staring at him. "You didn't have to discuss that."

"Nope, I didn't have to. It was my pleasure to," he said. "Besides, Ice told me about your fling with Catherine." And, at that, he chuckled and dug into his own dinner.

This concludes Book 4 of Bullard's Battle: Garret's Gambit.

Read about Kano's Keep: Bullard's Battle, Book 5

Kano's Keep: Bullard's Battle (Book #5)

Welcome to a new stand-alone but interconnected series from Dale Mayer. This is Bullard's story—and that of his team's. All raw, rough, incredibly capable men who have one goal: to find out who was behind the attack on their leader, before the attacker, or attackers, return to finish the job.

Stay tuned for more nonstop action as the men narrow down their suspects ... and find a way to let love back into their own empty lives.

Catherine. DeeDee. Paris. Kano had hoped to never deal with the three again. The woman he loved, her dragon of a mother, and a city to bring the best—and worst—memories to mind. A return trip leads to a conversation with DeeDee, which sheds more light on who is behind Bullard's murder in that planned plane explosion.

After seeing Catherine again, Kano can't stop thinking about her. That young woman matured into someone he couldn't have imagined and now can't forget. However, he's afraid her powerful mother is setting him up to die—yet again.

Catherine hadn't expected to see Kano again, but this time she's not letting him walk away. And she's prepared to face off against her snake of a mother to save him. Catherine must plumb the depths of her own soul and that of her family to save Kano—and herself.

Find Book 5 here!
To find out more visit Dale Mayer's website.
smarturl.it/DMSKano

Damon's Deal: Terkel's Team (Book #1)

Welcome to a brand-new series from *USA Today* best-selling author Dale Mayer, where dark-ops SEALs have special senses and skills, needed to solve intrigue, betrayal, and ... murder. A series with all the elements you've come to love, plus so much more, ... including psychics!

ICE POURED HERSELF a coffee and sat down at the compound's massive dining room table with the others. When her phone rang, she smiled at the number displayed. "Hey, Terk. How're you doing?" She put the call on Speakerphone.

"I'm okay," Terkel said, his voice distracted and tight.

"Terk?" Merk called from across the table. He got up and walked closer and sat across from Levi. "You don't sound too good, brother. What's up?"

"I'm fine," Terk said. "Or I will be. Right now, things are blown to shit."

"As in literally?" Merk asked.

"The entire group," Terk said, "they're all gone. I had a

solid team of eight, and they're all gone."

"Dead?"

Several others stood to join them, gathered around Ice's phone. Levi stepped forward, his hand on Ice's shoulder. "Terk? Are they all dead?"

"No." Terk took a deep breath. "I'm not making sense. I'm sorry."

"Take it easy," Ice said, her voice calm and reassuring. "What do you mean, *they're all gone?*"

"All their abilities are gone," he said. "Something's happened to them. Somebody has deliberately removed whatever super senses they could utilize—or what we have been utilizing for the last ten years for the government." His tone was bitter. "When the US gov recently closed us down, they promised that our black ops department would never rise again, but I didn't expect them to attack us personally."

"What are you talking about?" Merk said in alarm, standing up now to stare at Ice's phone. "Are you in danger?"

"Maybe? I don't know," Terk said. "I need to find out exactly what the hell's going on."

"What can we do to help?" Ice asked.

Terk gave a broken laugh. "That's not why I'm calling. Well, it is, but it isn't."

Ice looked at Merk, who frowned, as he shook his head. Ice knew he and the others had heard Terk's stressed out tone and the completely confusing bits and pieces coming from his mouth. Ice said, "Terk, you're not making sense again. Take a breath and explain. Please. You're scaring me."

Terk took a long slow deep breath. "Tell Stone to open the gate," he said. "She's out there."

"Who's out there?" Levi asked, hopped up, looked outside, and shrugged.

"She's coming up the road now. You have to let her in."

"Who? Why?"

"*Because*," he said, "she's also harnessed with C-4."

"Jesus," Levi said, bolting to display the camera feeds to the big screen in the room. "Is it live?"

"It is, and she's been sent to you."

"Well, that's an interesting move," Ice said, her voice sharp, activating her comm to connect to Stone in the control room. "Who's after us?"

"I think it's rebels within the Iranian government. But it could be our own government. I don't know anymore," Terk snapped. "I also don't know how they got her so close to you. Or how they pinned your connection to me," he said. "I've been very careful."

"We can look after ourselves," Ice said immediately. "But who is this woman to you?"

"She's pregnant," he said, "so that adds to the intensity here."

"Understood. So who is the father? Is he connected somehow?"

There was silence on the other end.

Merk said, "Terk, talk to us."

"She's carrying my baby," Terk replied, his voice heavy.

Merk, his expression grim, looked at Ice, her face mirroring his shock. He asked, "How do you know her, Terk?"

"Brother, you don't understand," Terk said. "I've never met this woman before in my life." And, with that, the phone went dead.

Find Book 1 here!

To find out more visit Dale Mayer's website.

smarturl.it/DMSTTDamon

Author's Note

Thank you for reading Garret's Gambit: Bullard's Battle, Book 4! If you enjoyed the book, please take a moment and leave a short review.

Dear reader,

I love to hear from readers, and you can contact me at my website: www.dalemayer.com or at my Facebook author page. To be informed of new releases and special offers, sign up for my newsletter or follow me on BookBub. And if you are interested in joining Dale Mayer's Reader Group, here is the Facebook sign up page.
https://smarturl.it/DaleMayerFBGroup

Cheers,
Dale Mayer

Get THREE Free Books Now!

Have you met the SEALS of Honor?

SEALs of Honor Books 1, 2, and 3. Follow the stories of
brave, badass warriors who serve their country with honor
and love their women to the limits of life and death.

Read Mason, Hawk, and Dane right now for FREE.

Go here and tell me where to send them!
http://smarturl.it/EthanBofB

About the Author

Dale Mayer is a *USA Today* best-selling author, best known for her SEALs military romances, her Psychic Visions series, and her Lovely Lethal Garden cozy series. Her contemporary romances are raw and full of passion and emotion (Broken But ... Mending series). Her thrillers will keep you guessing (By Death series), and her romantic comedies will keep you giggling (*It's a Dog's Life*, a stand-alone novella; and the Broken Protocols series, starring Charming Marvin, the cat).

Dale honors the stories that come to her—and some of them are crazy and break all the rules and cross multiple genres!

To go with her fiction, she also writes nonfiction in many different fields, with books available on résumé writing, companion gardening, and the US mortgage system. She has recently published her Career Essentials series. All her books are available in print and ebook format.

Connect with Dale Mayer Online

Dale's Website – www.dalemayer.com
Twitter – @DaleMayer
Facebook – facebook.com/DaleMayer.author
BookBub – bookbub.com/authors/dale-mayer

Also by Dale Mayer

Published Adult Books:

Bullard's Battle

Ryland's Reach, Book 1

Cain's Cross, Book 2

Eton's Escape, Book 3

Garret's Gambit, Book 4

Kano's Keep, Book 5

Fallon's Flaw, Book 6

Quinn's Quest, Book 7

Bullard's Beauty, Book 8

Bullard's Best, Book 9

Terkel's Team

Damon's Deal, Book 1

Kate Morgan

Simon Says... Hide, Book 1

Hathaway House

Aaron, Book 1

Brock, Book 2

Cole, Book 3

Denton, Book 4

Elliot, Book 5

Finn, Book 6

Gregory, Book 7

Heath, Book 8

Iain, Book 9

Jaden, Book 10

Keith, Book 11

Lance, Book 12

Melissa, Book 13

Nash, Book 14

Owen, Book 15

Hathaway House, Books 1–3

Hathaway House, Books 4–6

Hathaway House, Books 7–9

The K9 Files

Ethan, Book 1

Pierce, Book 2

Zane, Book 3

Blaze, Book 4

Lucas, Book 5

Parker, Book 6

Carter, Book 7

Weston, Book 8

Greyson, Book 9

Rowan, Book 10

Caleb, Book 11

Kurt, Book 12

Tucker, Book 13

Harley, Book 14

The K9 Files, Books 1–2

The K9 Files, Books 3–4

The K9 Files, Books 5–6

The K9 Files, Books 7–8

The K9 Files, Books 9–10

The K9 Files, Books 11–12

Lovely Lethal Gardens

Arsenic in the Azaleas, Book 1

Bones in the Begonias, Book 2

Corpse in the Carnations, Book 3

Daggers in the Dahlias, Book 4

Evidence in the Echinacea, Book 5

Footprints in the Ferns, Book 6

Gun in the Gardenias, Book 7

Handcuffs in the Heather, Book 8

Ice Pick in the Ivy, Book 9

Jewels in the Juniper, Book 10

Killer in the Kiwis, Book 11

Lifeless in the Lilies, Book 12

Murder in the Marigolds, Book 13

Nabbed in the Nasturtiums, Book 14

Lovely Lethal Gardens, Books 1–2

Lovely Lethal Gardens, Books 3–4

Lovely Lethal Gardens, Books 5–6

Lovely Lethal Gardens, Books 7–8

Lovely Lethal Gardens, Books 9–10

Psychic Vision Series

Tuesday's Child

Hide 'n Go Seek

Maddy's Floor

Garden of Sorrow

Knock Knock...

Rare Find

Eyes to the Soul

Now You See Her

Shattered

Into the Abyss

Seeds of Malice

Eye of the Falcon

Itsy-Bitsy Spider

Unmasked

Deep Beneath

From the Ashes

Stroke of Death

Ice Maiden

Snap, Crackle...

Psychic Visions Books 1–3

Psychic Visions Books 4–6

Psychic Visions Books 7–9

By Death Series

Touched by Death

Haunted by Death

Chilled by Death

By Death Books 1–3

Broken Protocols – Romantic Comedy Series

Cat's Meow

Cat's Pajamas

Cat's Cradle

Cat's Claus

Broken Protocols 1-4

Broken and... Mending

Skin

Scars

Scales (of Justice)

Broken but... Mending 1-3

Glory

Genesis

Tori

Celeste

Glory Trilogy

Biker Blues

Morgan: Biker Blues, Volume 1

Cash: Biker Blues, Volume 2

SEALs of Honor

Mason: SEALs of Honor, Book 1

Hawk: SEALs of Honor, Book 2

Dane: SEALs of Honor, Book 3

Swede: SEALs of Honor, Book 4

Shadow: SEALs of Honor, Book 5

Cooper: SEALs of Honor, Book 6

Markus: SEALs of Honor, Book 7

Evan: SEALs of Honor, Book 8

Mason's Wish: SEALs of Honor, Book 9

Chase: SEALs of Honor, Book 10

Brett: SEALs of Honor, Book 11

Devlin: SEALs of Honor, Book 12

Easton: SEALs of Honor, Book 13

Ryder: SEALs of Honor, Book 14

Macklin: SEALs of Honor, Book 15

Corey: SEALs of Honor, Book 16

Warrick: SEALs of Honor, Book 17

Tanner: SEALs of Honor, Book 18

Jackson: SEALs of Honor, Book 19

Kanen: SEALs of Honor, Book 20

Nelson: SEALs of Honor, Book 21

Taylor: SEALs of Honor, Book 22

Colton: SEALs of Honor, Book 23

Troy: SEALs of Honor, Book 24

Axel: SEALs of Honor, Book 25

Baylor: SEALs of Honor, Book 26

Hudson: SEALs of Honor, Book 27

SEALs of Honor, Books 1–3

SEALs of Honor, Books 4–6

SEALs of Honor, Books 7–10

SEALs of Honor, Books 11–13

SEALs of Honor, Books 14–16

SEALs of Honor, Books 17–19

SEALs of Honor, Books 20–22

SEALs of Honor, Books 23–25

Heroes for Hire

Shane, Book 12

Diesel, Book 13

Jerricho, Book 14

The Mavericks, Books 1–2

The Mavericks, Books 3–4

The Mavericks, Books 5–6

The Mavericks, Books 7–8

The Mavericks, Books 9–10

The Mavericks, Books 11–12

Collections

Dare to Be You...

Dare to Love...

Dare to be Strong...

RomanceX3

Standalone Novellas

It's a Dog's Life

Riana's Revenge

Second Chances

Published Young Adult Books:

Family Blood Ties Series

Vampire in Denial

Vampire in Distress

Vampire in Design

Vampire in Deceit

Vampire in Defiance

Vampire in Conflict

Vampire in Chaos

Vampire in Crisis

Vampire in Control

Vampire in Charge

Family Blood Ties Set 1–3

Family Blood Ties Set 1–5

Family Blood Ties Set 4–6

Family Blood Ties Set 7–9

Sian's Solution, A Family Blood Ties Series Prequel
  Novelette

Design series

Dangerous Designs

Deadly Designs

Darkest Designs

Design Series Trilogy

Standalone

In Cassie's Corner

Gem Stone (a Gemma Stone Mystery)

Time Thieves

Published Non-Fiction Books:

Career Essentials

Career Essentials: The Résumé

Career Essentials: The Cover Letter

Career Essentials: The Interview

Career Essentials: 3 in 1

Made in the USA
Coppell, TX
14 March 2022

74966071R00134